Diary Of A 12 Inch Brotha!

A Novel

CELEBRITY PUBLISHING
UNLIMITED

Disclosure

This is a work of fiction. Names, character, places and incidents are products of the author's imagination or are used fictitiously. Any resemblance to actual events or locales or persons, living or dead, is entirely coincidental.

ISBN# 13: 978-0-9798047-0-0
ISBN# 10: 0-9798047-0-1

Cover Model: Logan Steffon
Typeset/Inside Layout: Linda Williams

DANTE' FEENIX:

"Sex and Relationships Expert"

Join me on the Examiner.com for some indepth articles & interviews! I get up close and personal; trust me… YOU"VE NEVER SEEN REPORTING LIKE THIS! Log on:

www.examiner.com

www.facebook.com/dantefeenix

www.dantefeenix.com
to join my email list today!

Printed in Canada

Diary Of A

12 Inch

Brotha!

"ARE YOU IN THE CLUB?"

By

Dante' Feenix

CELEBRITY PUBLISHING UNLIMITED

Irina,

Hello my Newest friend...

Ms. Eyes!! Enjoy the

Erotic climactic master-piece...

Dedication

This book is also dedicated to the people that tried to stop it from coming out. You know who you are…

To My FANS and Supporters:

Thank you for all the love and support! This novel was not possible without your constant emails and requests. Thank You for the book signings, the digital sales and overall genuine love. People have tried to hold me back in this arena but your support saw me through. Once again… Thank You.

THE 12 Inch Brotha WOLF PACK: Logan Steffon(Thanks for your support over the years, you believed in me beyond bounds), Larry Mc.(My Sense of Family), Andre G.(My Craziness) Uncles Calvin B.(My Cool), Leroy T.(My Advice), Grady M.(My conscious), **My homies:** Anthony Allen Osborne, Darric Boyd, Dulane Barnes, Laron Lambert(cuz), Ray Burton(cuz), and anyone I missed. Sorry ladies, this one is for the men! Blame it on my mind not my heart. **Last but not least** my best friend in the world and inspiration for writing My Son DJ(I loved you before you were even born!)

My fallen soldiers: Marty Boston, Kurt, Floyd Roberts, and Thomas White.

*****Get Up Close and Personal** with Hip-Hop Business Journal's author of the year, **DANTE FEENIX**, by subscribing to his articles on The Examiner! He is the **SEX & RELATIONSHIPS** expert for Baltimore. Just log onto http://www.examiner.com and enter his name to get all the articles. "It's free and it's all me; I really get personal on the Examiner!" –DF/x

Diary Of A 12 Inch Brotha!

Dear Reader,

As I wrote this erotic novel it dawned on me that most people may miss the point because of the title or its graphic nature. So without spoiling the pleasure of self discovery for anyone, I'd like to offer some food for thought that hopefully you will keep in mind as you read the book. It's called **4 Girlfriends!**

Once upon a time (Yes, I did say that)… there was a MAN who had four girlfriends.

He loved the **4th girlfriend** the most, adorned her with rich robes and treated her to the finest of delicacies. He **gave her the best!**

He also loved the **3rd girlfriend** very much and was always **showing her off** to everyone. However, he feared that one day she would leave him for another.

He also loved the **2nd girlfriend**. She was his confidant. She was always kind, considerate, and patient with him. Whenever this guy faced a problem he could **confide in her** and she would help him get through the difficult times.

The man's **1st girlfriend** was a very loyal partner and had made great contributions in maintaining his wealth and life. However, he **did not love the first girlfriend** although she loved him deeply. He hardly even took notice of her.

One day, the man became gravely ill and knew his time was short. He thought of his luxurious life and became worried. "I have four girlfriends with me now but when I die I'll be all alone."

So he asked the 4th girlfriend, "I have loved you the most, endowed you with the finest clothing and showered great care over you. Now that I'm dying, will you follow me and keep me company?"

"No way!" replied the **4th** girlfriend and she walked away without another word. Her answer cut like a sharp knife right into his heart.

The sad man then asked the 3rd girlfriend, "I loved you all my life. Now that I'm dying, will you follow me and keep me company?"

"No!" replied the **3rd** girlfriend. "Life is too good! When you die, I'm going to marry someone else!" His heart was broken and turned cold.

He then asked the 2nd girlfriend, "I have always turned to you for help and you've always been there for me. When I die, will you follow me and keep me company?"

"I'm sorry, I can't help you out this time," replied the **2nd** girlfriend. "At the very most, I can only walk with you to your grave." Her answer struck like a bolt of lightning and the man was devastated.

Then a voice called out: "I'll go with you. I'll follow you no matter where you go. I will never leave you!"

The man looked up and there was his **1st girlfriend**. She was very skinny because she suffered from malnutrition and neglect. Greatly grieved; the man said, "I should have taken much better care of you when I had the chance."

In truth, we all have 4 girlfriends in our lives:

Our **4th girlfriend** is our **body**. No matter how much time and effort you lavish in making it look good, it will leave you when you die.

Our **3rd girlfriend** is our **possessions**, status and wealth. When you die, they will all go to others.

Our **2nd girlfriend** is **our family and friends**. No matter how much they have been there for us, the furthest they can go with us is up to the grave.

Finally, our **1st girlfriend** is **our Spirit**. It's often neglected in pursuit of wealth, power and the pleasures of the world. However, your Soul is the only thing that will follow you wherever you go. Cultivate, strengthen and cherish it now because it is the only part that will follow you and continue with you throughout Eternity.

Remember, "When life pushes you to your knees, you're in the perfect position to pray." Now, enjoy this novel!

Much Love,
Feenix

PS. – You can get all Feenix books on AMAZON Kindle _months early_ *for under $5.00! Get a Kindle now!*

I wanna kiss you…
Until your clothes fall off.
I wanna use your ass like an oxygen mask
Until you… pull- me –off!

I wanna grab you by the waist
and grind you to a better place,
Then go deep sea diving…
and come up with a shiny face!

Can I kiss the back of your neck
and tell you, baby… I missed you before you left?
Then watch you cry before you cum
and tell me, "Ba-by you're the fuckin- best!"
At this…
Now, you're gonna just have to take my word for it
because them bitches will cut you…
If you try to check my references!

I'm as bad as I wanna be
The five fingers of death are me.
I'll lift your hood if it's all good,
so I can gently circle parts of your anatomy….
Who's bad as me?
Baby, I can do whatever it takes to please
because I got it swingin' at the knees,
you should call me your Invincible Luva!
But when I'm through… you'll be page 32,
in "Diary Of A 12 Inch Brotha!"

-Thicke Rique da Ruler

Introduction

"Ladies Night!"

"Come on Tina, damn! We gonna miss the show!"

"I can't find my cell phone Niagara. What if Sam tries to call me?"

"So what! He knows you're out with me, shit. Long as it took us to get here; you shoulda noticed it was missing before now. I'm tryin' to get in da club before we miss somethin, girl!"

"A'ight hoe, but what if he gets mad at me?"

"He'll just have to get over it! Besides, we never hang out anymore. You need some me time tonight, girl. You know what I mean?"

"Aw hoe, you ain't really interested in hanging with me. You just tryin' to see that Thicke Rique dude since your mister wonderful mystery man dumped your ass!"

"Aw, now that's some fucked-up shit to say. He didn't dump me; we're just taking some time off."

"My fault; I'm only serious. Ha! You're not usually the sensitive type. What's up with you, Niagara?"

"Nothing that seeing a little... oops, I mean a lot of dick can't handle," said Niagara while she puckered her lips, snapped her fingers, and twisted her body like a bad stripper.

Both girls laughed as they ran from the parking lot to the front door of The Swingin' Cable Club. Niagara was a fair-skinned, tall, and slim knockout; with huge breasts and a tight ass. She liked to work out regularly, a good habit that she developed from serving four years in the army reserves. Her friend Tina however, was a petite brown skinned ghetto cutie with a short haircut and a bodacious body. She never worked out but wore a body shaper to help her achieve a figure much like Niagara's.

They frequented the male exotic dance scene in their hometown of Richmond, Virginia as a way of breaking the monotony of normal life. Lately however, Niagara had been hearing about how off the chain the dancers were at The Swingin' Cable Club in Washington, DC. Especially their Dee-Jay and star performer, Thicke Rique da Ruler, who was the main attraction and chief reason she wanted to go. Niagara needed to see if all the hype was true since she had recently been dumped by her booty call boyfriend of two years.

By the time they made it to the lobby of the club, both Niagara and Tina were excited. Everything was purple and black trimmed in gold, like royalty. All you could hear was loud music over the sound of women laughing and having a good time. A black curtain with a sign that read *Beware of the O-Zone* draped the entrance to the main floor. After paying the ticket girl, Niagara and Tina were given a small bottle sprayer filled with scented oil and water.

"What the hell is this for?" Tina asked as Niagara giggled in the background.

"For you to get the dancers wet in the O-Zone," the ticket girl quickly replied.

"That's not the only way to get them wet. Oops, did I say that out loud? Off to the hoe zone Niagara!" Tina blurted out as Niagara anxiously pulled her through the black curtain to the main floor.

"Dayum," both girls said in unison.

They stood together blocking the entrance to the main floor as Adore by Prince played loudly over the speakers. The club was extremely sexy and set-up differently than most. From the entrance you could see the layout of the whole club. The Dee-Jay booth looked more like a pedestal because it was suspended in mid air on Roman columns. The main area was an elevated circle like structure with the focal point being a pit dead center. Plus, there were tables and chairs scattered all around so you could order food and watch the show from a distance if you wanted to.

"Come on girl, so we can get a good seat up close and personal!" Niagara continued to pull Tina's arm until they reached a table at the edge of the pit. Once there, they could completely see the finale performance area with black and purple laced bed-like structures spaced out with huge over sized satin pillows. Yes, it was definitely the O-Zone!

"Damn, that has got to be the hoe-zone," said Tina.

"It's O-Zone Tina, not hoe zone," Niagara responded while shaking her head.

"Oh yeah? Just wait until we get in that motherfucker, ho-o-o-o-o!"

Both Tina and Niagara started snapping their fingers and dancing like rookie strippers, until... at that moment, the lights went low and the music changed from Adore to the big bass sound of the old school hit *Don't Turn Out The Lights* by the World Class Wrecking Crew. Smoke filled the club as a tall figure entered the spotlight of the Dee-Jay pedestal to the roar of women randomly shouting, "Thicke Rique, Thicke Rique!"

"Oh girl look, there he is... There go your baby daddy, Niagara!" Tina and Niagara laughed like two fifteen year olds with a high school crush.

"Shut the hell up, girl. He's about to go behind the turntables. Damn, he sure is fine."

"Fine? Bitch, you better stop tryin' to fall in love and go get that soul pole! Look at all these hoes in here. They got him on their radar... I can tell."

"Yeah right, they a'int the ones I need to worry about," Niagara joked.

4

Diary Of A 12 Inch Brotha!

"Shi-it, I aint gonna lie. I wouldn't mind gettin a little piece of the rock, you can call me miss Prudential. I'd limp my black ass all the way back home to VA with a big smile on my face! "

"Tina, you are crazy as hell and let's not forget... married too."

"I know, but my husband probably wouldn't even be able to touch the sides after that shit. I heard his dick is so big he leaves an echo behind, girl. Hello, Hello, Hell-o! Can anybody hear m-e down ther-e?"

Ha, Ha, Ha!

"Okay, now I'm really not fuckin' with you anymore Tina. Be quiet hoe, he's about to say something."

"Ladies! Are you ready to see some hard bodies?" announced Rique to the sea of women.

"We ready to see yo' body nigga," yelled Tina.

"Shhhh Tina, are you gonna act like this all night?"

"You damn right. Until I get some good dick in my life, I'm not cooperating with anybody!"

Rique began to speak again, "Hello ladies, I'm Thicke Rique da Ruler, part owner of 12 Inch Brotha Incorporated. I would like to welcome you to The Swingin' Cable Club! Up first we have the Mandingo Triangle; Big Mac, Officer Friendly, and my main man, Donnie Cock-erin in his legal brief-s!"

The crowd screamed with excitement and as the night progressed, Niagara kept trying to make eye contact with Rique. She was waiting for the right moment to strike! Even though she told Tina it was her first time at the club; she had been there before but never made her presence felt. Women at the clubs in Virginia would tell many stories about Rique and how smooth he was. How he would sweep women off their feet and fuck them like something in a movie.

Most women she knew would never admit how much they needed or desired something like that, but Niagara was sexually and romantically frustrated so she was wide open to the idea. A fairy-tale like that was exactly what she needed in her life, especially after all the drama she'd been through with her ex. You see, Tina was more of a talker while Niagara was a do-er! So if this man was all that women said he was; she fully planed on taking that dick for a little test drive around the block!

"Tina, look at those pretty eyes; those sexy lips, and them thick eyebrows. Mmm, I can hardly sit still."

"Fuck that! Girl, look at his chest and the print in dem jeans. Mmm, Mmm, Mmm! I'm about to go up there and squeeze it."

"Yeah right. You sure talk a lot of shit Tina, because truthfully speaking... you got the perfect man at home in Sam. I'm just keeping it one hun-ned."

"Yeah, you're right Niagara. I love my husband to death, girl. Ain't no mountain high enough, Ain't no valley low enough... Um, what's his name again," Tina said jokingly and laughed so loud, people turned to look.

"Aw, shut the hell up hoe! You know Sam is a good man," said Niagara.

"Well at least that sentence rhymed, maybe you should be a rapper... Sam is a good man," Tina mocked then continued, "Look Niagara, he's coming down from the Dee-Jay booth!"

Niagara sat at her table and watched the man that was the object of so many women's desire head towards the bar. "He's probably an asshole," she mumbled to herself while tuning Tina totally out. "Shit, I'm only hoping he's an asshole to save myself from doing what I know I'm going to do if he's not."

"Huh? Bitch, what the hell are you mumbling about over there," asked Tina.

"Nothing, mind your business Tina! Dang, why are you all over here and thangs. I'll be right back; I'm going to the bathroom."

"Yeah right... if I'm not here when you get back, I might be lost in the Man-dingo Triangle. Woo!"

Niagara followed Rique with her eyes as he stood at the bar to order a drink. She could see other women pointing at him, so if she was going to make her move it would have to be now. Niagara inched her way over to the bar just behind him, leaned over his shoulder, and told the bartender to give her the same drink he was having. She then squeezed herself into the space beside Rique at the bar and said, "Hi, how are you? That drink sure looks good, what is it?"

"They call it Cranberry Juice... " He didn't even turn to look at her. Immediately she was embarrassed and could tell from his tone that he was in fact an asshole as she suspected.

When the bartender brought her cranberry juice over, she paid him and apologized to Rique for intruding. Before she could get the hell out of dodge, he grabbed her wrist gently and said, "You didn't let me finish. I always drink cranberry juice when I don't have a friend to drink with." He smiled then continued, "Would you be my friend and share some Grey Goose and cranberry with me?"

Niagara's pussy clinched one time as she answered, "O... Okay."

"Bartender! Get me and my new friend..."

"Oh, my name is Niagara."

"Niagara, some Grey Goose to go with this cranberry juice... and add a bottle of Hypnotiq." He continued to smile while she nervously tried to create a conversation.

"So, you're the Dee-Jay here, huh?"

"Shhh, don't tell anybody because I'm trying to keep that a secret," jokingly said Rique.

"Yeah, I know that's a silly question," she replied.

"I'm just joking around, of course I'm the Dee-Jay and you are the most adorable thing I've ever seen in a BeBe shirt and a pair of jeans."

Niagara smiled; she couldn't understand how she went from hating this guy to blushing in a matter of seconds.

"I'm sorry, I don't mean to sound corny but you caught my eye as soon as I got into the Dee-Jay booth. I wanted to give you a compliment before I have to go back. Have I seen you here before?"

"No," she responded while flirting with her eyes.

"Are you sure? I'm normally pretty good at remembering faces."

"Maybe it's not my face you would remember."

Rique chuckled and said, "Maybe not."

Anxious to change the subject Niagara leaned in cleavage first and said, "Maybe it was my big... bright smile?" She had a few jokes of her own, "I'm just kidding but I didn't think what you said was a corny line, after hearing some of the things I hear on a daily basis I thought it was actually quite sweet. So thank you."

"You're more than welcome, but you have to excuse me if I seem a little out of it tonight. I'm really tired and I don't even get out of here until about two o'clock," said Rique while yawning.

"Aw, it's only about 10 o'clock now. How long does it take for you to get home?"

"About two hours, if I drive the speed limit. I live near the Maryland and Delaware border in Elkton."

"Well don't take any chances if you're too tired to drive, maybe you should get some rest first. Do you have a place in the back where you could lay down for a few?"

"Thanks, but you can't get any rest around here during clean up. People are yelling and rushing to get out of here. I might ask big sis if I can jet early tonight."

"Your sister? Aw, he needs his big sister's permission, that's so cute. Does she have your pajamas with the feet in them too?"

"Ha, Ha, so you got jokes I see. No, my sister is my road manager and partner... for your information. She stays backstage during the shows to keep an eye on everything. So, are you having a good time little miss smarty pants?"

"Um…Um…yeah, it's alright."

"Aw, hopefully by the end of the night it will be a little better than just alright. I'll tell the guys to step it up okay? I have to go back now adorable, thanks for sharing a drink with me. The bill has already been taken care of."

As he walked away Niagara had so many things she wanted to say but only mumbled, "Woo! He can get it."

"Ladies, give it up for The Mandingo Triangle! They'll be back for The O-Zone later on tonight! If it's your first time here at The Cable, do me a favor and clap your hands!" Niagara clapped her hands up high as she received dirty looks from the women that saw her talking to Rique at the bar.

"I welcome you to The Cable where we give you time to eat, have fun, and enjoy the show first! Then at the end of the night, you can take a trip down to the O-Zone in the center pit and spray your favorite dancer! Get him all soaking wet and slippery! Sound good? This is not just another club, it's an amusement park! So make sure you get on all the rides and don't forget me… The Big Dipper!

"Oh shit! I heard that," yelled Niagara in the direction of the stage.

"Alright everybody, it's time to get back to business! But before I do…I'd like to send a kiss to my adorable new friend who's having just an alright time tonight. Muah! Don't worry baby because I'm about to bring out my main man, Raaa-aaam Rooo-ck!"

"Damn bitch! You gonna stand over at the bar all night and just let me sit there by myself lookin' stupid?" Tina came out of nowhere and startled Niagara, she was a little pissed-off.

"I'm sorry Tina, but damn..."

"You see... that's why I don't fuck wit bitches no more because ya'll always act crazy when you come up on some new dick!" Tina said angrily with her hand in the air. She was definitely making a scene, which Niagara hated so she tried to calm her down.

"Aw girl, don't act like that. I was just talking to him and trying to see what he was like?" Niagara poked her lip out like a baby.

"Well... what's he like?"

"Girl... my pussy is about to jump out my draws. He's sexy as hell but I can't put my finger on why," said Niagara while staring aimlessly.

"Put your finger on what? Girl, take a good look at him... damn. Plus, he supposed to be packin' a fat one too. Please, what's there not to like?"

"No, it's not that. He seems confident, intelligent, and he knows how to talk to a lady."

"So where's the lady?" Tina laughed to herself and slapped her own knee before she continued, "How you got all of that out of five minutes of conversation, I'll never know. But don't make this more than it is, just ride that dick into the sunset and get it over with!"

"Shut up girl."

"Look, I'm not stupid. You didn't drag me out the house, drive way up here, and pay all that money just to see a show and have a conversation. You should have seen your face when he first stepped on the Dee-Jay thingy. I said to myself, that nigga's done... literally!"

Ha, Ha, Ha!

"Come on hoe, before somebody takes our table." Niagara was a little agitated by Tina because she always put a negative spin on things.

"Ooh my goodness Niagara, is this our Hypnotiq?"

"He already paid for it, so I guess so... drunky."

"Girl, that's my shit. I love Hypnotiq."

"Your drunk ass would love anything right now... don't touch this bottle Tina! You've been drinking all night and you can't mix that stuff you had with this. It's gonna make you sick," said Niagara in a firm tone as if she was scolding Tina for not knowing when to stop.

"My one night off husband house arrest and you gonna act like you're a member of MADD or something. Mothers Against Drunk Driving and shit!"

"That's right Tina; because you can't hold your liquor. Look at you... already messed up and I'm supposed to let you take this whole bottle? Yeah right, not gonna happen captain. "

"That's it; I've had it with your ass! Soon as I get home I'm starting my own club called D.A.M.M!"

"DAMM? What's that stand for?" asked Niagara.

"Drunks Against Mad Mutherfuckas... like you!"

"Ha, Ha, now I know your ass is drunk. I don't care what you do but you are not getting this bottle. This time, I'm going to the bathroom for real and mister Hypnotiq is coming with me." Niagara was through playing with Tina because she was getting messy drunk and she hated to see her like that.

When Tina got back to their table, she saw a lot of drinks. A line of five lemon drop shots, another bottle of Hypnotiq, and two more glasses of what she had been drinking all night. She immediately figured out who sent them and held the first shot up to the Dee-Jay booth. Tina then drank the other four back to back.

Rique smiled at her from the booth and said, "Damn... don't hurt nobody baby," on the microphone. Tina opened the bottle of Hypnotiq and walked over to the back stage area. The security refused to let her back where the dancers were without an escort. But of course Tina wasn't having that, especially in her given state.

"I don't care if they got their dicks out! I'm just tryin' to thank the Dee-Jay because he sent me and my friend some drinks."

"I'm sorry miss, but I can't let you back there without an escort." The bouncer explained.

"An escort? Alright, well you take me back there to see the Dee-Jay then. Since you take your job so damn serious and won't let me..."

"I got her Greg, she's with me." Rique came from behind the backstage curtain with his shirt open and grabbed Tina by the arm. She was swaying from side to side as if she was about to fall.

"Yeah Greg, chill the fuck out," Tina said drunkenly as they went backstage.

Once behind the curtain, Rique looked deep into her eyes and said, "How are you doing, baby? Were you looking for me or one of the dancers?"

"First of all, how are yo-u doing mister Thicke? My name is Tina. Me and my girlfriend came all the way up here from Virginia and yes, I was looking for your fine ass." Tina smiled as she tried to keep her balance. "I just wanted to say thank you for the drinks and errthang. Plus, my girlfriend…"

"Wait a minute baby; let's get out of the backstage entrance because I can't hear you that well." Rique took Tina to a dimly lit private room backstage. "You can finish talking; I have to get ready to go out on stage a little bit later."

"Wait, you dance too?"

"Yeah, just in the grand finale though." Rique grabbed his G-string and started taking off his pants. "But you go right ahead and finish what you were saying."

Tina began to stutter, "I- I- I thought it was really nice that you had brought us drinks and all. I was telling my girlfriend at the bar how sexy and fine you were…"

"Oh, so you think I'm sexy?" Rique stood up with nothing but his boxers on and his G-string in his hand. His stomach and every inch of his body was cut and well defined. He didn't look that big in clothes but his body was rock hard and he looked like walking sex to Tina. Rique began to slowly walk toward her.

"Yeah, you sexy as hell and if I wasn't marri…"

"Tina, I really need your help with something," Rique cut her off. "Every night before we go onto the stage we have to tie-up. That means I have to jerk off and tie myself right under here..." Rique reached into his boxers and pulled out the biggest dick Tina had ever seen in her life. She couldn't believe he was still soft. Tina was so drunk that all she could do was keep nodding her head okay and licking her lips.

"I wanted to know if you could help me get it how it needs to be, baby. Would you do that for me? Help me out little," Rique whispered softly.

He placed his hand on the side of her face and she automatically started to sink as if on an elevator going down. Rique put his dick lightly on the crevice of her mouth so she would have to reach out with her lips to get it. Tina began licking the tip and rolling her eyes as Rique softly placed his hand on the top of her head.

"Get the balls," he whispered as he lifted his dick while Tina kissed down the shaft to begin lightly sucking and licking his sack. She could feel him growing as she cupped his balls with one hand and grabbed his dick with the other. It felt enormous to Tina as she put her mouth over the head again and began to really work.

Knock, knock, knock!

"Wait a minute... damn. I'm in here right now!" Rique pulled his dick out of Tina's mouth and it made a popping sound. He lifted Tina to her feet and said, "Look baby, we gonna have to speed this shit up. Pull your jeans down; I want to put it between your thighs so I can cum." Rique had already started unbuckling her jeans, so all she had to do was just assist him with getting them down her thighs.

Tina loved how gently assertive Rique was. Once down, he put his dick right at the tip of her pussy. The only thing between them was the thin material of her thong. As Rique pumped Tina moaned, wanting this new dick inside her. She grabbed his powerfully muscular shoulders and tried to lift her leg but it was caught in her jeans. Maneuvering herself only made it worst because she could feel his dick throbbing between her thighs and on her pussy. She could not believe the strength of this man lifting and holding her up the whole time, it was like something out of a movie.

All at once, Rique stopped without cumming. His dick was hard as granite and her pussy wouldn't stop throbbing as if it was saying please don't go.

"I have to get back; I'm a real private person so wait about ten minutes before you leave. I'll have Donnie come get you and escort you out. If you ever come again, we can get together more privately and finish what we started?" Tina smiled and nodded as Rique began to bite on her neck and shoulders while he grabbed his pants.

"What about your G-String?" she panted.

"I'm going to the bathroom and put it on so I can wash myself; your pussy got me wet as a muthafucka."

When he left, all she did was quiver and think of the best way she could get back to the club another day without Niagara. After waiting a few minutes, Tina exited the private room.

"Shit, I ain't got all day to be waiting for somebody to come get me. I'm missing the show," complained Tina.

When Tina came from backstage Niagara was arguing with the same bouncer that had previously stopped her.

"She's okay Greg, don't throw her out," yelled Tina with a smirk on her face.

"Greg? How in the hell do you know him? I've been out here looking for your ass for like an hour and shit. Then you come out here talkin' about some, she's okay Greg! Where the hell you been and how you know him like dat? " Niagara was losing her patience with Tina.

"Girl, I just went back there to thank your boy for the drinks he had sent us to the table. Why you actin all crazy and shit," asked Tina while she struggled to maintain her balance.

"Cuz that's some bullshit! You just wanted to leave me since I left you. Girl, Rique is not thinking about your little ass. He was in the Dee-Jay Booth and I still didn't see your groupie ass anywhere."

"Groupie ass... Oh really? Are you sure about that?" Tina's eyes bulged.

"Yeah, really! For some strange reason you always seem to jock the niggas that like me, must be some ol' Single White Female type shit." Niagara rolled her eyes at Tina and looked in another direction.

"What? You need to check yourself because you're really about to put your foot in your mouth, for real." Tina began to get increasingly angrier.

"Whatever, I'm not talking about it anymore. The finale is about to start." Niagara started walking to the table as Tina laughed to herself and shook her head while following.

"Ladies, it's that time once again! Grab your spray bottles, your money, and a change of panties! It's time to get a seat in the O-Zone! Each dancer will come out in five minute intervals until they're all on the floor. You can freak them, tip them, and wet them! So let's get it started with my main man the magnificent, Tongue Fu!"

Tina grabbed her purse and spray bottle, "I'm going down there." Niagara was still pissed with Tina, so she continued to roll her eyes and ignore her."

Tina joined the other women in the pit and waited for Rique to come out. "He's not thinking bout me huh? Well her ass is about to get a bird's eye view… spoiled ass hoe," Tina whispered aloud to herself. She was drunk out of her mind and tired of feeling like Niagara's sidekick. Tina always drove, waited for Niagara to get ready, and had to listen to her stories for hours. Well not this time, she was finally going to show Niagara that she was nobody's sidekick.

As the finale progressed and the dancers came out one by one, Tina partied the night away all over the O-Zone. Niagara decided to go back to the bar and leave her number for Rique with the bartender.

"Are we having fun yet," asked a deep sexy voice from behind. Niagara turned to look and it was Rique!

"I am now Mr. Sexy," she purred.

"The club owner and my sister said it was cool for me to leave now. I told them I was tired and didn't really feel well, but I'm actually getting a room at the hotel across the street."

"Oh, that's nice. So this is the last I'll see of you tonight huh?"

"Well, it doesn't have to be. I definitely could use some company across the street. I was kind of hoping that my new friend would tuck me in tonight?" Rique smiled with his pearly white teeth.

Niagara wanted to say yes badly, but knew that it would be a total hoe move and she didn't have a way home afterwards.

"My girlfriend drove so I don't really have a way home if I don't leave with her tonight. Plus, I don't wanna feel like one of your many groupies." Niagara didn't really care about looking like a groupie but wanted to see how Rique would respond to the groupie statement.

"What's wrong with being a groupie? I'd be one for you; as a matter of fact I am your groupie. Would you sign my chest please?" Rique pulled his shirt open and chuckled seductively for a moment then said, "I'm just playing but if you change your mind call me. Here's my cell number. I'm going to get my things and leave out the back door, see you later adorable.... I hope." Rique didn't even address the groupie comment further than the joke because he hears it all the time.

He knew most women loved men that other women wanted so feeling like a groupie in a weird way could be a turn on if done right. Rique leaned over and gave Niagara the softest kiss she ever felt on the side of her face, grazing her neck. But before he could leave, she grabbed his arm and said, "Now you know that little kiss was not even fair."

"My cell will be on all night, I'm hoping you'll come get the rest. Give me a call if you want to cum... oops, I mean if you're coming over. If not, I still want you to call and let me know that you got home safely, okay adorable?" Rique smiled again in an attempt to woo Niagara. She smiled back at him and nodded yes but was thinking more like hell yes... no wasn't even an option.

After Rique left, Niagara sat at the bar drinking Hypnotic in big gulps and imagining how she would fuck the shit out of him. As she downed her last glass she stood, looked in the mirror behind the bar, and said to herself, "Well, looks like I'm going to be a hoe tonight. Don't judge me!"

Niagara was laughing as she walked down into the pit of the O-Zone. She could see Tina in the corner with her legs wrapped around one of the dancers getting pounded.

"Tina! Tina!" Niagara grabbed her arm as she was being jerked back and fourth by the dancer.

"Oh Ni-ag-ara girl, I am so sorry a-bout ar-gu-ing wi-th yo-u!" said Tina as her voice vibrated from the pelvic trauma she was receiving.

"Never mind that Tina, but you don't have to take me home tonight!"

"What?" Tina looked at Niagara. "Stop... I said stop!" She yelled and began to pull away from the dancer's grasp. "Now, what did you say Niagara?"

"I said I'm ok for tonight, I'm going to stay here!" Niagara held one ear because it was so loud in the pit.

"Where and who is going to bring your ass all the way back home to Virginia?"

"Tina, don't start. I'm a grown ass woman and I'm in DC all the time."

"What grown got to do with it? We came up here together and we gonna leave here together! I knew this shit was gonna happen!" Tina was getting angry all over again.

Niagara began to make excuses, "Look... both of us been drinking, I can't drive, and we both know you can't drive. Shit, you can barely walk for that matter."

"Girl, I can't stay up this muthafucka... I'm married! Sam would have two babies and a cow if I stayed out all night," yelled Tina.

"Oh, so now you're married all of a sudden. What about a minute ago? I'm sure Sam won't say nothing if you just call him and say that we drank too much," replied Niagara sarcastically.

"What? You are sadly mistaken because he will flip the fuck out! I'm goin' home tonight, I can drive. You just want to stay up here with somebody. I hope it's not Mr. Thicke or whatever his name is."

"Yes it is, but that's besides the point..."

"No, that's exactly the point. You got me all the way up here, talking about girls' night out and shit. Soon as you find some dick to lay up with, you try to leave me. That's the shit I'm talking about right there. You got me out here arguing on the dance floor, O-Zone or whatever the hell you want to call it! This is fuckin' bullshit!"

"Look Tina, this conversation is over. You're not gonna embarrass me out here, point blank! I'm not getting in the car with you tonight, you're drunk, I'm drunk, and that's that! If you want to take your life in your own hands, go right ahead but I am staying here." Niagara made her statement firmly as she attempted to put her foot down and bring the conversation to a close.

"What bitch? Get the fuck out of here with those stupid ass excuses, plus you're being dumb as hell because he was trying to fuck me backstage anyway!" Tina decided to play her trump card.

"Yeah right, with your hatin' ass. Why in the world would he be trying to fuck you when he..." Niagara laughed.

"When what? Go ahead say it...When he could have you? I should fuck you up behind that shit!" Tina got in Niagara's face.

"But you're not," said Niagara as she turned quickly and walked away from Tina. She knew the situation was about to get ugly and that would only delay her rendezvous. The security from the club saw the two women arguing and began to move toward them through the crowd.

"Little red whore, that's why that other nigga left your ass!" Tina yelled from across the room and prepared herself for a fight.

Niagara quickly turned and walked back up into Tina's face and said, "What the fuck did you say to me?"

"I said... that is why that rich nigga you were fucking dropped your ass for another bitch after he got you pregnant!"

Niagara grinded her teeth then whispered in Tina's ear, "I will fuck you up if you ever mention him to me again." She turned and quickly walked away again because she could see the security approaching.

"Oh yeah!" Tina yelled as she raised her fists and swung at Niagara from behind. "Bitch, don't try me!"

Tina hit Niagara on the side of the face and off to the back of her head before the bouncers could grab her arms to restrain her. Niagara fell forward; she was embarrassed by all the drama so she stayed low and made her way through the crowd. Once in the clear she ran out of the club and headed to meet Rique.

Meanwhile, Rique had already checked into his usual room at the hotel. He knew the entire night crew of Dominican workers that affectionately called his room "La noche última espectáculo" or the "Late night show." Between duties they would take bets on whether the women Rique took to his room would be fuerte jode or "loud fucks." He had built quite a following among his Dominican brothers who referred to him as "Sammy Sosa del dormitorio" or "The Sammy Sosa of the bedroom."

When Rique sat on the bed in his room he placed a call to his main squeeze Shyla and left a message on her voicemail. He began to reflect on the night's previous activities, which immediately brought Tina and Niagara to mind. Rique laughed to himself because these two were classic examples of how competitive and cut throat women can be with each other.

He's said it a hundred times... One of the easiest ways to sleep with an attractive woman without obligation is to make her feel she's competing with other women, especially a friend. Then the sex is not even about you, it's about her winning.

Rique had to record this in his journal or diary as most people liked to call it. However, he didn't like to refer to his journal as a diary because it was fundamentally different in his opinion. A diary keeps track of daily events and is a way for a person to self-counsel or feel that they are talking to someone. That's where you get the term, Dear Diary. It's like you are telling someone how you feel and that's the last thing Rique ever wanted to do. He hated talking about his feelings.

His journal was more of a poetic account of issues and people he encountered during his life as a dancer. He didn't write in it every day and definitely didn't want anyone else to read it. In his opinion, the journal contained too much knowledge and truth that the world, especially women, was not ready to hear but needed to. For instance, Niagara and Tina illustrated one of those truths crystal clear... female rivalries.

"Today's entry will be dedicated to my Virginia honeys... Tina and Niagara. I'm gonna call it Girl-friends."

Diary Of A 12 Inch Brotha!

Entry #101: Girlfriends

Girlfriends, Girlfriends, Can you really trust them?

Oh yeah? What about when it comes down to men?
Before you say YES ask yourself, what kind
of friend have you been? Did you say,
Loyal and supportive?
Yep, they're the ones that usually get done in.
I can tell you right now… every woman has
one friend their man knows he can SWIM IN…
and back stroke in her deep end!
Even though every woman knows, which home
girl is the hoe… they still call her,
"Girlfriend."
So before you make some chick your road dog,
your bosom buddy, or your Siamese twin…
make sure you've checked her ass at the door,
or that shit might bite you in the ass at the end…
"Girlfriend."

Chapter I

"Blaque' & The Doc"

A few weeks later... Blaque, Rique's sister and the daughter of John and Shirley Barbee, decided to increase her visits to the family psychologist. She was a spoiled ass, strictly business minded, young woman with control issues. Blaque' wanted to totally control all aspects of her life which included you, if you were a part of it. That was her major problem with keeping friends, lovers and family... especially her brother Rique! A great looking, very well endowed man that found his enjoyment between women's legs. His twelve inch dick made him the object of desire for many women and a lucrative business opportunity for his sister.

Diary Of A 12 Inch Brotha!

"Okay Blaque', I need you to explain one more time what's upsetting you so badly?" asked Dr. Joyce, the family psychologist, during Blaque's bi-weekly sessions.

"I don't know Doc; it's just not the same anymore. My brother Rique is so unfocused right now and he's not handling business the right way! I think he's forgotten why we're here because he's letting these hoes run him!"

"The hoes are running him?" Dr. Joyce chuckled slightly, "What does that mean?"

"It means he's unfocused because of women. Check this out; he's got one chick on a leash that's nothing but drama and another that he will immediately drop anything for. Both of them are a pain in my ass and I wish they would disappear. They are messing up everything that my brother and I have built together."

"You're talking about Niagara and Shyla again, right?"

"Yep, that's them. Niagara is a bootleg bag carrying, fake ass Beyonce wanna be, that keeps popping up everywhere! I mean damn, doesn't this bitch have a life? You know what I'm saying, doc? I hate to see a woman play herself for a man like that."

"By playing herself, you mean…"

"Wait In The Car Bitches! That's what I like to call them. It's when a man only likes you because you're so convenient and submissive to him. A booty call chick, but one step better because he doesn't just call her at night; he calls her whenever he's bored or needs something. Most of the time men like to use these bitches to run errands, kick out doe, and fuck on command."

"Your brother has swagger like that?" asked Dr. Joyce.

"Pleas-e... let me finish. The funny thing is that these types of women think that they are actually spending time with the man when he doesn't really want to be seen with them. So whenever he takes the woman anywhere... for whatever reason... he says, Wait in the car, I'll be right back. That's a wait in the car bitch! Stupid ass hoes..."

"Sounds like you've had some experience with that..." implied the doctor.

"Bull-shit!" Blaque' interrupted. "I'm not even gonna let you finish that statement Doc because I know that you are too smart of a woman to ever think some dumbness like that about me. All those degrees on that wall over there, should at least give you the insight to know better than that. I'll fuck a nigga up quicker than a hero sandwich at a weight watchers convention, if they try that with me!"

Dr. Joyce chuckled to herself because Blaque''s eyes bulged with outrage as she spoke. She always found it easy to push Blaque''s buttons when it came to men. "Okay, I'm sorry. I was only kidding. However, I still don't understand why you're taking this so personal."

It's not that I'm taking it personal; I don't like this particular chick or women like her. Did you ever see Flavor Flav's show, Flavor of Love when it was on TV?"

"Yes, I've seen the show once or twice," replied Dr. Joyce as she smiled and nodded her head.

"Well, on the very first season there was a girl named Hoopz that won the whole thing."

"Yes, I remember her."

"Do you know that bitch Niagara had the nerve enough to say that people mistook her for Hoopz but she has a better body? Bullshit, I told her that she looked more like Oops... with her wack ass weave. Like the hair dresser kept sayin' oops bitch, oops!"

Ha, Ha, Ha!

Blaque' held her stomach while she laughed and began to slide off the couch.

"Okay I get the picture, you don't like the type of woman Niagara is. What about Shyla? During our last session you said that she was nothing like Niagara but she's messing everything up as well."

"Not messing everything up, I said fucking everything up! There's a big difference ya know."

"No, I didn't know that. Why don't you tell me the difference Blaque'?"

"The reason I used the term fuck up instead of mess up is because a fuck up is more intense than a mess up. Most people never recover from fuck ups but mess ups are easy to correct. With that in mind, let's take first things first... the bitch is married!

What's worse... is that he drops everything when she calls! I mean everything like; private parties, club dates, travel arrangements, and all other money making opportunities! He changed his whole act because one time she came to the Cable Club and got mad at how he was all up on the women. Hello? That's his job dumb ass. He's a fuckin' stripper... oh, and a Dee-Jay."

"Whoa, wait a minute. She's married and he gives her that type of priority?"

"Hell yeah, that bitch is married. Don't act like you don't see married people cheating all the time Doc."

"Yes, I guess you're right but during our other sessions you made it seem like she was his main squeeze."

"She is! That's the problem! He gives this hoe so much priority that he has missed several private parties that I had specifically booked for him and numerous other engagements. When she calls it's like nothing exists, his mind shuts down!" Blaque' put her head down and shook it from side to side in disappointment.

"I can see that this really bothers you unlike the other girl whom you simply don't like very much. Other than the money you've already lost, do you think that she is leading your brother down a road that could hurt him or get him hurt?"

"Nah, he's a big boy. He can take care of himself on that end, but I do think that she makes him think about getting out of the business."

"What? That sounds awfully selfish Blaque'."

"Selfish? I take care of that boy Doc. Without me he probably wouldn't even make it out here in this cold ass world! He was a mediocre Dee-Jay before I got involved; tenth on every clubs calling list. It was me that took him from $250 to $1500 a gig plus tips, his own dance troop, and one hell of a lifestyle I might add. I believed in him before anyone else did! So what do I get for it? I'll tell you what, nothing! It's like he doesn't even know what the word loyalty means anymore."

"I know you think you're right, but again I ask, don't you think that's being a little selfish? What about Rique? Blaque', your brother's probably very confused both mentally and emotionally judging from what you tell me. I mean you're his sister right? Shouldn't you care?"

"Yeah I know, but I can't help but wonder why Shyla is so special? He has tons of women throwing themselves at him all the time. Believe me, I would know. I don't know if you've heard Doc, but the boy is blessed... if you know what I mean."

"Yeah I know what you mean Blaque'. Your brother is well endowed and that's basically how you came up with the name for your business, 12-Inch Brotha Incorporated. You're using a play on words based on the size of his penis to cross market the Dee-Jay and exotic dancing aspects of your business. That's pretty smart, if I do say so myself."

"Penis...you're so funny Doc, can't you just say dick once? Yes, the whole concept was my idea, so thank you. You see, he started as a plain old Dee-Jay limited to old school parties and family functions until I got him a regular gig on male stripper night at the local club.

He grew to be quite popular, so one day I decided to go with him. I saw that the women were simply in love with him but of course he was fucking most of them by that point. They would hang around the Dee-Jay booth all night long trying to see who was going to get a piece of dick for that night... simply pa-thetic!

The real problem was that these bitches were giving the strippers all their money and not my brother." Blaque' chuckled a little then continued, "Let's re-cap, fucking my brother but paying other dudes? Oh no, these bitches got it twisted. Let's get that money! So I pulled Rique to the side and the rest is history! Now we have our own dance troop and make money from everyone, even the club owner."

"Sounds like you've turned him into a male prostitute to some degree," said Dr. Joyce with a very apprehensive look on her face.

"Ha, Ha, Ha... very funny Doc. I knew them degrees weren't on your wall for nothin." Blaque' laughed out loud and clapped her hands together because she enjoyed alarming Dr. Joyce. It was her way of getting back for all the previous smart comments.

"I'm kidding doc. You should have seen your face! No, we are not doing anything illegal; we're just getting money from dancing. If anything, he's pimped himself a long time ago."

With a very concerned look on her face Dr. Joyce said, "Is money the only thing that's important to you?"

"Is there anything else, doc? I mean, security is always an important issue to every woman and money definitely represents a form of security. "

"Does this fear have anything to do with your childhood?"

Diary Of A 12 Inch Brotha!

"I wouldn't call it fear, it's more like insurance. You have car insurance right?"

The doctor nodded yes, anxiously awaiting Blaque''s response.

"So would you call that a fear of accidents or just wise planning? Plus I told you before; I don't want to talk about my childhood because to me…"

The doctor interrupted, "Point taken… but all I was saying is that in the last session you shared with me that you knew that your bother was your mom and dad's favorite. This might be the reason security is so important to you, it could be stemming from some form of an abandonment issue."

"Whatever the fuck ever… I don't even speak to my father or mother. As far as I'm concerned they're dead to me and I'm dead to them. If you want to know anything about them ask my brother."

"I would love to speak to him, but you said he absolutely would never meet with me in a million years."

"Yeah, I bet you would like to meet him." Blaque' leaned forward. Do my stories of his numerous women and huge dick make you hot Doc?"

"You know what Blaque'… I break a lot of my own rules to have these sessions with you. I never let a patient curse as much as you do during a session, we usually run over our time, and I even moved other appointments around so that you can get the Fridays you want. So please don't tempt me to drop you as a patient by disrespecting me any further with your comments."

"Alright Doc! Point taken, besides he hates shrinks... oops, I mean psychiatrists anyway. Let's talk about you... where are you from Doc because I know you're not from here?" Blaque' smirked as if to hold her laughter back.

"Toronto. Okay, that will end our session for today. But can I ask you one more question Blaque'?"

"At your own risk! I'm just joking Doc. Go ahead, spit it out."

"During our past sessions, you kept bringing up the fact that your brother always writes in a little journal or book. Have you ever read it?

"Umm?" Blaque' rubbed her chin as she thought about why the doc was really asking this question. She didn't even get a chance to reply before Dr. Joyce hit her with another question.

"Oh yeah, one more thing Blaque'... Why don't you ever take notes or write anything down from our sessions?"

"Actually, that's two questions Doc. Remember, time is limited! But no, I don't read his shit... any of it! It's probably just about some of his hoes and sexual escapades anyway. Secondly, I don't write anything down because all of this is bullshit and that's what I pay you for, right? To listen to my bullshit, write it down and sort it all out for me."

"Again you disrespect me by cursing Blaque'!" Dr. Joyce stood with a stern look on her face.

Buzz!

The secretary's voice came over the intercom as the tension in the room got thick between the two women.

"Dr. Joyce, Miss Melanie is here to pick up Miss Blaque'."

"Oh my, look at the time… saved by my best friend in the whole wide world once again." Blaque' smiled at Dr. Joyce and began to scoot pass her. "Thanks again for seeing me Doc; we'll do this again next month… toodles."

As Blaque' left the building the doctor looked puzzled and said to her self, "Why is she so increasingly disrespectful toward me? Is it possible for me to help her if she can get under my skin as much as I can hers?"

Dr. Joyce Vee was one of the best psychiatrists in DC, but for the first time in her career she is at a loss for words. She sat back in her chair and began to use her hand held digital recorder.

"Patient 066, Blaque' J. Barbee. In this session the patient seemed to be so self centered that she created her own reality and then reacted to it. I've noticed an increase in verbal aggression as she felt a need to challenge me for her own reasons. Blaque' seemed to be totally obsessed with money and survival on a level that is beyond my understanding. She appears to use her brother as a vehicle for her own success and security.

Chapter II
"Business Meeting"

"Come on Melanie, please. It's only a quick meeting, twenty to thirty minutes tops and we out! Dalvin won't care, besides it's not like the club is open during these hours anyway." Blaque' attempted to convince her best friend Melanie to accompany her to a weekly meeting with the dancers.

"Alright Chas, I'll go in this time but you gotta understand that I'm not trying to embarrass my man. Things are different now, I could just see the magazine articles... Washington Wizards star Dalvin The Truth Melody's wife was seen leaving a male strip club. They would never say in a million years that it was in the middle of the day before the club opened to attend a business meeting with her friend."

"Correction, Melanie! It will read; his pregnant wife... was at the strip club!" Blaque' laughed out loud then hugged Melanie before she could move away.

"That was not funny at all, Blaque'. I would just die if I harmed his career. Girl, you don't think that someone..."

"No I don't," Blaque' interrupted. "I would never have you do anything that puts your marriage in jeopardy. You and Dalvin are the only reasons I still believe in real love. I'll make the meeting quick if you promise me that you won't put your new name on your license... Melanie Melody. That shit sounds crazy as a hell!"

Laughing hysterically like teenagers, Blaque' and Melanie went into the Swinging Cable Club where both she and Rique were going to have their weekly meeting with the dancers. Everyone was already waiting on Blaque' because she was very strict about being punctual to these meetings. 12 Inch Brotha Incorporated was growing to be one of the east coast's most popular male exotic dance revues.

"Alright girl scouts, listen up... No more bitches back stage unless you are getting paid!" Blaque' liked to shock everyone into paying attention. She knew that her male dancers saw women in a powerless light for the most part. So she made sure they didn't get her confused with the customers.

"If you gonna fuck a bitch... do it on your own time, not my dime! Beat your shit, like everybody else in the free world, to the magazines in the back closet when you gotta beef-up. These bitches ya'll bring to the back are starting to get on my damn nerves because they think that they are special." Blaque' made it a point to make eye contact with each and every dancer as she spoke to let them know she wasn't playing.

"Besides the fact that I might fuck one of them up for getting smart with me, I will fire your ass! We don't have time gentlemen for female or male bullshit! It hurts the money... and when you hurt Ben, you hurt me."

Melanie leaned over and whispered in Blaque''s ear, "Who the hell is Ben?"

"Who in here can tell my best friend Melanie who Ben is?" Blaque' asked the men at the meeting.

"Benjamin Franklin, as in the president on the hundred dollar bill," said the club owner from the back of the room.

"Tony, I knew you would get it! But do the rest of ya'll girl scouts get it? Money is why we are here... not pussy!"

"But some of us get most our money from pussy," Officer Friendly, a male dancer jokingly interrupted.

Blaque' smiled while everyone laughed at Friendly's comment, "As long as I get my percentage... I don't give a fuck what you do. However, most of you don't even know how to do that correctly, so let's keep it simple. I wasn't going to say any names but you asked for it... Friendly."

"Now see, all that ain't even necessary," said Officer Friendly.

"I'll tell you what's necessary, not the other way around," Blaque' replied sternly.

Everyone began to laugh hysterically as Officer Friendly walked out of the meeting noticeably angry. Blaque' closed the meeting, looked at Melanie and said, "He'll be alright, cuz he ain't even trying to see my cousins come up here. He better ask somebody that knows me." Anyone that challenged Blaque' in any way would be made an example. When it came to business or the streets, she had no seeable weaknesses.

As Blaque' and Melanie left the club they noticed what appeared to be a long swipe across the side of Melanie's BMW.

"What the fuck? Melanie, look at the side of your car!" Blaque' yelled as they both ran to the vehicle.

"Somebody side swiped my car!" Melanie's voiced cracked as if she were about to cry.

Blaque' scanned the whole parking lot with her eyes to see if anyone was around that could have seen what happened. Unfortunately, no one was outside at the time.

"What a fucked up thing to do. I'm so sorry sweetie; people just don't care anymore. They'll hit your shit and keep going on about their business. I try to tell you that all the time, Mel." Blaque''s attempt to console Melanie wasn't helping.

"Shut the hell up Chas, not now... please. This is the third time in a few months something like this has happened to me... ever since Dalvin gave me this car. He is going to get pissed and say that I'm driving his insurance premiums up. Am I really that irresponsible?" Melanie put her face in her hands and shook her head while Blaque' hugged her.

"He'll understand Mel. Don't get the baby all upset over some bullshit car." Blaque' opened Melanie's hands and made a funny face as they touched heads.

"Yuck, ever since we were kids I hated when you would make that ugly face," Melanie pulled back then she giggled with Blaque'.

"Dayum! What happen to your car Melanie?" Officer Friendly and Ram Rock shouted in unison as they left the club.

Blaque' immediately jumped to her friend's defense, "What does it look like? Somebody hit it, assholes. Mind your own damn business unless you going to kick in some money or a spare ride." She stretched her eyes wide, twisted her lips, and stared them down while Ram-Rock and Officer Friendly walked by looking the other way.

"Yeah, that's exactly what I thought... make tracks. Niggas always got something to say until you bring up money."

"Blaque', leave them alone. They are only showing some concern about what's going on."

"No they ain't! They want to giggle about it later like a couple of little girls. That's what I mean; you're always trying to make everyone noble in your mind. I'm going to say this one more time from the cheap seats...

people don't give a fuck about you Melanie! They could care less about you or your situation. Look at your car, who ever hit it is probably somewhere chillin right now. Let's call the police and get a report."

Melanie pulled out her cell phone and called the police while Blaque' examined the spot where the car was swiped. She ran her fingers down the side of the vehicle and pulled away some of the paint from the other vehicle.

"Purple? Girl, I think you got hit by Barney or some shit. Who in the hell would be driving around in a purple car. Oh snap, maybe you got hit by Prince." Blaque' started licking her hand and dancing. She was trying to make Melanie laugh.

"Girl, sit your silly self down. The police said that they would be here in a minute. I want them to take this seriously." Melanie couldn't stop herself from smiling at Blaque''s antics.

Chapter III
"Sexsational"

"Ladies, thank you for joining us once again at the Swingin' Cable Club! Give it up for all the dancers one more time!"

It was an average night at the club; everyone clapped and whistled frantically when the dancers walked back onto the stage one by one. Rique was tired but anxious to get to his next destination so he tried to wrap the show up quickly.

"We enjoyed playing with you this evening and we'll be back next time for some more fun. I'm Thique Rique Da Poet and as always, we want you to cu-m again… and again, and again. What the hell, you can even bring a friend! You get the picture... until next time; satisfy yourself if you can't depend on no one else!"

Rique exited the stage and quickly went to his dressing room to grab his jacket. Blaque' had already collected the door money and began collecting her percentage from the dancer's tip money in the back meeting room.

"If you have gotten drinks for yourself or any of your little freaks tonight, make sure you settle your tab before you leave! The club makes money off the bar and I don't want Tony to come looking for my ass because of you! Plus, some of ya'll are still coming up short because you do not give a good enough show. FYI... get it together boys or I will replace your sorry asses!"

"Hey Blaque', where's Rique?" asked one of the dancers as they all got dressed in front of her. Most of them were secretly vying for her attention because they were so use to getting it from women all their lives. Now here they were... dick swinging and exposed, but this women didn't seem to care at all. If Blaque' wasn't a pimp, she sure was well on her way to becoming one.

"That's a good question," Blaque' replied suspiciously. She walked to Rique's dressing room but saw him in the hallway with his bag.

"Where the hell are you going? We haven't even counted tonight's take," she said angrily.

"I'm sure you got that covered, I'm tired and ready to go. I'm staying at the hotel across the street tonight so jot the breakdown on a piece of paper and give it to me with my share of the money."

"See, now that's the shit I'm talking about. Chasing pussy and not taking care of business first. Who is it, Niagara's crazy ass?" Blaque' stood in his way demanding an answer.

"Mind your business girl; I'll be at the hotel. Just holla at me on my cell phone when you are done." Rique pushed by Blaque' as she turned and began to yell at him.

"You are giving it away for free when we should be getting paid for it! Not smart Rique, not smart at all!" Once at the hotel, Rique immediately felt the urge to write in his journal about that night's much anticipated return visit from Niagara. Rique sat on his hotel room bed and wrote:

Entry #102: "Sexin' A Star!"

A... mazing I do agree, with every word I write
My mind speaks in 3-D. More recently...
"I Love You" has been lost at sea,
because for years baby, it's been lost in me.
So sexy...
Sex me with your search light of ecstasy,
Maybe you can "Rescue Me,"
So don't worry too much about my recovery.
I tend to recover quickly... because
I'm confident and Sure! Like I'm the 84' Al B.
However, with you I choose not to...
Through you maybe I could learn a lot, Boo.
Like, You can't climb the highest mountain
without risking the greatest fall."

Diary Of A 12 Inch Brotha!

and "What would summer heat be without
the cool relief of the fall?"
So tell me,
What kind of man would I be if I didn't answer the call,
Of my body parts once you've kissed them all?
Plus, I know you're not
gonna punch a clock, Once you've felt
the greatest "cock" of them all.
And I might not be Tupac...
But I'll give you "Thug Life" up against the wall,
Or look into your eyes as I super size you in the back of my car.
So don't be surprised when you see the sunrise
without me...
Because you've been sexin' a star!

After fully settling up for the night, Blaque' made her way across the street to the hotel where Rique was staying. She knew the front desk personnel well so it was nothing to find out his room number. As she approached the room she tried the door before knocking and found that it hadn't shut all the way. She busted in the room and immediately started fussing at Rique.

"I hope you're not wasting our money on this hotel room! Whatever freaks you got lined up for tonight better be payin for this shit!"

"Damn, how the hell did you get in?" Rique responded startled, in a semi-angry tone.

"Don't worry about it. A damn army could walk up on you when you're writing in that little diary of yours."

"Look Blaque', I told you to stop calling it a diary. It's not a diary... that shit pisses me off and you know it!"

45

"Oh get over it; you're such a candy ass about that damn book. What I really want to know is… if the company is paying for your little hotel sex-capdes."

"Don't even start with me because I've got that covered. But if I did decide to pay for the room, it would only be with my share of the money so mind your damn business. Plus, you need to get out of here because I'm about to take a shower anyway."

"Boy please, ain't nobody worrying about you. Those hoes must really get you gassed up! I've been seeing your little skinny naked ass since we were kids. I just wanted to get the money straight before the hoe patrol rolls up in this mutherfucka."

"Ha, Ha, very funny Blaque'." Rique went into the bathroom, turned on the water, stripped, and hopped into the shower.

Buzz, Buzz, Buzz!

"Damn!" Rique jumped back out the shower and ran to get his cell phone. "Hello… Shyla? Thanks for callin me back so quickly, can you talk right now?"

"Not that married ass bitch again," Chasity said angrily.

"Yeah Rique, I got a minute. Make it quick though, my husband will be home soon," replied Shyla.

Rique's other line began to beep, but he didn't click over because he didn't recognize the number.

"Well, I was calling because you said that we might be able to hook up soon."

"Yeah, maybe tomorrow baby, but I'll have to call you back. You know my husband is crazy jealous. I got to get off this phone." Shyla was noticeably nervous.

"Okay, I'll leave my phone on. You better not have me sitting around here and waiting all damn night like before."

"You're so silly. I didn't tell you to wait... you chose to."

Rique could tell she was smiling at that point. He knew she liked when he appeared desperate for her and in some ways he was because he could never totally have her.

"What? You told me that once you had finished what you were doing you was going to..."

Shyla cut Rique off before he could finish his statement, "I gotta go. He's pulling into the garage, talk to ya later baby."

Click!

Rique stared at his phone for a minute with a look of disbelief on his face. Almost instantly his phone began to buzz again after the call with Shyla abruptly ended. It was the same strange number from before.

"You are dumb ass shit!" Blaque' chuckled as she fell against the wall. "Chasing her all around town, dat bitch don't give a fuck about you."

Rique ignored Blaque''s insults about Shyla as usual and said, "Damn, somebody's blowin me up. Oh yeah... I think I know who this is."

Rique answered in a deep laid back tone, "Hello?"

"Hey sexy."

"How you doin sweetie?" Rique answered but he wasn't one hundred percent sure it was Niagara.

"Not very good... got a lot on my mind right now and needed to release some stress. So, I wanted to know if you could fill that order," requested Niagara.

Rique smiled to himself because he was now sure of whom it was. "No problem, just come to the hotel across the street from the club. I'll come down and meet you in the lobby."

"Alright, I'll be there in a minute. Are you going to make me feel like your groupie again?" Niagara smiled seductively while she held the phone waiting for his answer.

"I think I can handle that if you are willing to play a few games tonight girl." Rique bit his lip as he spoke to Niagara on the phone because he knew that it would annoy Blaque'.

"Oh, I already started. You can't tell? I was waiting for you to catch up." Niagara was quick on her feet when it came to seductive comments.

"Woo! Girl, you better get that little thang over here and let the games begin. I'll see you shortly."

Click.

Rique quickly dried off and threw on his sweat pants. He didn't bother putting on any boxers because he wanted to get straight to business. Rique figured that Tina had told Niagara about their encounter by now, so she had to like being a groupie if she was going to keep fucking him. He pulled out the condoms as usual and sat them in plain view so that he wouldn't be tempted to take a little dip in the pussy raw dog.

Soon as Blaque' saw him set the condoms out she shouted, "Oh no, I'm getting the fuck outta here! You need to leave that other bitch Shyla alone though. She ain't nothing but trouble. I'm not going to keep telling you that until you get sick of hearing it."

"Well, now would be a good time. I wish you would stop giving me advice about my Lil Shy-Shy because that's my ba-by! Now, can you leave and stop blockin please?" Blaque' left and Rique sprayed cologne on the bed and in the vents. He then turned the hot water up in the shower and left the bathroom door open so that the room could be filled with steam when he returned with Niagara.

When the doors to the elevator opened Rique could see her standing at the front desk of the hotel with the fattest ass he had seen in a while poking out from under a lightweight black hipster wrap jacket. She was wearing a black cat suit with heels and a black men's hat slightly tilted in the front like Alicia Keys in the video for Fallen. Rique smiled and slowly walked up to Niagara while having visions of bending her over the air conditioning vent in the room later on.

"Hey you... are you waiting for somebody special?" Rique began to set up a role he wanted to play with Niagara, "because if he doesn't show up... I definitely got you baby."

"Yeah... I'm waiting for my new friend, but you're so sexy I might have to go with you instead," said Niagara seductively.

"Oh, you got jokes? Ha, Ha, Ha! What's up sweetie, have you been waiting long?"

"No, but I'd wait all night for you. I'm surprised there's not a line of women down here the way they were acting at the club the other night."

"Nah, I told you I'm a private person." Rique walked Niagara over to the hotel's front desk. "Hey Jerry, what's the deal son?"

"Nothing much Rique, are you going to take care of this now?"

"Oh, my sister slash so called manager didn't tighten that up before she left?"

"No, nobody came by here but this young lady. I need a credit card, you know how it works."

"Damn, I didn't bring my card downstairs with me because my sister was supposed to take care of all this. I got it upstairs so it's not really a problem. Sweetie, you got a credit card on you?"

"Yeah, but I don't know how much I still have...."

"That's okay he's not gonna charge nothing on it. I'm gonna use my card to close out, it's just in case we use the phone or something. You know how it works."

"No problem baby, I got you." Niagara reached into her purse and gave the front desk clerk her Visa card.

"Why don't I give you the money upstairs and be done with it?" Rique asked.

"Whatever is easier for you I guess." Niagara shrugged her shoulders then said, "It's really not a big deal, as a matter of fact this time's on me."

"You heard the lady Jerry, here you go. I'm going to make it up to her when we get upstairs." Rique smiled at Jerry as he gave him the card.

Jerry had a smirk on his face as if to say, I'm sure you are. He's seen Rique do this a million times and was still amazed at how much it worked. Women may lust for Rique, but it's the men that seemed to idolize him.

"Okay, Sammy! I'll take care of everything," Jerry exclaimed.

As Niagara and Rique headed back to the room everyone kept speaking to Rique as if he were a celebrity.

"Sammy!"

"What up Jesus," Rique smiled as he walked by.

"Hey Sammy! Who's the lovely lady man?"

"None of your business Juan! Go back to work man." Rique imitated his accent then laughed.

Niagara giggled. She thought they were cute and liked all of the attention "Why do they call you Sammy?"

"I don't know, maybe it's Spanish for Rique. Girl, I'm just focusing on you right now." Rique hurried Niagara into the elevator before the damn workers could say anything else to blow his cover.

Rique's biggest turn on was a good girl that liked to be a little bad at times. He could always tell by what they drank, who they were with, how they dressed, and most of all their conversation. He was never into the straight up whores and Niagara was definitely a good girl with a bad streak according to his calculations.

Rique tickled and played with Niagara all the way to his room so that he could get the physical contact going early. When they got to the door his dick was already hard because of all the frolicking, so he pressed it up against her back and ass. Niagara stood in front of Rique while he made fake attempts to get the key into the lock. Rique began to kiss the back of Niagara's neck as she let out a sigh and pushed her ass back forcefully against his dick. Rique whispered in her ear and said, "How wet is your pussy right now?"

"Ummmm, wet enough to take it all this time."

"When I open this door, I want you to take off every fuckin' piece of clothes you have on. I'm going to eat that pussy up in the window seal."

"What if people see…"

The door flung open and Niagara stumbled into the room before she could finish her statement. The room was dimly lit by the moonlight shining through an open window, with steam and the smell of Rique's cologne everywhere. Niagara walked to the bed and sat her purse down as she attempted to comment, "Dang, you got it all dark in…"

Abruptly, Rique grabbed her from behind with his left hand firmly holding her around the waist while the other slid gently down the front of her pants rubbing her pussy ever so gently. At that moment, Niagara could clearly feel Rique's hard and now pulsating dick pressing up against her through his sweat pants.

Chest to back, he began to kiss her neck again and again while pushing her forward to the window. Niagara's eyes and neck began to roll as she grabbed the window seal to prop her ass up towards Rique, allowing his hand the full motion to continue rubbing her clit more vigorously.

"Take this shit off," Rique said in a firm but sexy tone. As Niagara took her arms out of the garment and rolled it down, he grabbed the cat suit from the sides and began to help her roll it down her thick thighs. Rique began kissing, biting, and licking from her ass to her calf while helping her to step out of the garment. After Niagara completely took it off he turned her around, kicked her shoes out of the way, cupped her ass, and began sucking on her breast enthusiastically. Niagara fell back into the window seal as he continued to give her some of the sweetest taboo she has ever known.

"I want to watch you play with yourself... lick your nipples and rub that pussy for me," whispered Rique as he walked over to the nightstand, opened the box of condoms, and stripped totally naked. His body looked like a perfectly chiseled sculpture that was accented by shadows and the moonlight from the window. Niagara started rubbing her pussy in quick circles as she watched him attempt to roll the condom down his enormous dick. She hurried over to him before he could complete the task, grabbed his hand and said, "Let me get that for you."

Niagara kneeled on the bed with her back arched and put her mouth over both the condom and the tip of

Rique's dick. She began to suck and roll the condom down his shaft as far as it could go.

"Uhhhhh," Rique let out a moan as his dick continued to grow and pulsate in Niagara's mouth. She in response gently rubbed his balls then turned her hands in a circular motion around the shaft of his dick as she went up and down.

Rique was pleasantly surprised by Niagara's skill level but soon began to wonder; Damn... Is she a professional? Laughing to himself as his head fell back to enjoy the treat, it soon became time for the main event.

Rique pulled his dick out of Niagara's mouth and softly used his hand to raise her chin upward. She sat up on the bed and he turned her around to begin rubbing her clit in soft circles from behind. Rique placed his dick on Niagara's ass while he simulated fucking with periodic powerful thrusts through her thong. Simultaneously, he continued to rub her clit and gently bite her neck until her thong was saturated.

Niagara closed her eyes and kept pushing back against him while she moaned from anticipation. Though Niagara was extremely wet, Rique still grabbed some warming KY Jelly. He rubbed it on the tip of the condom before he moved her thong to the side and began to slide his dick into her pussy from behind inch by thick inch.

"Ohhhhh my goodness!" Niagara sighed passionately as she clinched the covers on the bed. Rique was sure not to give it all to her in the beginning because that was reserved for just the right moment. He began to fuck her with the first few inches of his dick so that he could assess what she liked and keep it feeling good at the same time.

"You want me to stretch that pussy for you again? Huh baby? Tell me how much you love this dick Niagara."

"Yes... Yes..." breathing heavily, Niagara loved when Rique talked dirty to her and decided to get in on the fun. "Yeah, stretch that pussy daddy... stretch it! Fuck it... Fuck me... Fuck me!" Rique looked at her in shock as he continued to fuck her from behind with a larger portion of his dick.

He thought to himself, Oh she talkin' shit now? I'm gonna have to bring the pain. Rique wasn't used to that because most women were usually too busy gasping for breath and squirming away. He pulled his thick curved dick out of her, flipped Niagara over onto her back, and pulled her thong totally off. Dick in hand, he got between her legs and began fucking her with the tip escalating to about eight inch thrusts. He was so thick she could feel every inch go in; it made her jump because she could feel it deep in her abdomen. Rique reached under Niagara's legs and gently grabbed her wrist as he teased her with just the tip. He then lifted himself off the bed and began a repetition of full length grinding circles.

While breathing increasingly heavy. Niagara said, "Oh shit, that's it. Right there baby. I'm cummin Rique, baby I'm cummin, s-s-shit....."

Rique tightened his grip on her wrist so that she couldn't run away from him and began to thrust with the full length of his dick deep inside of her pussy. "Oh shit Rique... Sssssss! Uhh, Uhh, Uhh, Uhh, Uhh...."

"Say I love your dick Mr. Thicke. Say I love this dick!" Rique whispered forcefully. He began to bang her pussy in an upward motion as the slap from his balls on her ass intensified.

"Oh Shit... Mr. Thicke I love your dick! Oh, Oh, I love your dick. Its so thick, fuck... Ohhhh!"

As Niagara came Rique stopped pounding and released her wrist. He began to grind slowly while gripping her shoulders tightly, arching his back and digging deeper. Her legs kept bending then stiffening like a board over and over again until she was exhausted. Rique stood up off the bed and Niagara's legs continued to quiver uncontrollably.

Chapter IV
"Deeper"

"Hey Little Bits, what's going on? I'm missing you like shit. Give me a call to let me know when we can get together this week."

The next morning after Niagara left, Rique texted a message to Shyla's cell phone. Shyla was mixed with Black and Asian, petite, athletically built, and had very sexy legs. Rique anxiously awaited her call as he lay across the bed. They usually met about twice a week, but here lately she seemed to have been putting him on the back burner.

His feelings for Shyla. or Shy-Shy, as he liked to call her; had grown at an unusual pace which was not good.

Shyla was definitely a party girl with no real direction in life and on top of that ironically, she was married. That fact never mattered in Shyla's mind however; she acted like it shouldn't matter to Rique at all. She never looked at things from another person's perspective, which meant she felt that only Rique benefited from their relationship while she took all the risk. She was selfish but he still loved her.

In an attempt to keep his mind occupied until Shyla called back, Rique began to write about her in his journal.

Entry #103: Number One Contender

I miss you…
SOMETIMES even before you're gone. Clouded
scenes of passion, play for me, the sweet melody,
of your hypnotic song. Though, the
feelings are strong, I know I'm wrong,
Longing, for another
man's treasure, As the candlelight… shines
bright, to silhouette your edible thong.
You See,
I'm the number 1 contender.
And with every "thrust" of this love…
I'm plottin' your surrender.
I'm willing to die to take you. Is he willing to
cry to keep you?
Ask these questions and learn a painful lesson,
that your man is see through.
Glass,
But our love making is spiritual… like, morning

Diary Of A 12 Inch Brotha!

mass.
My hypnotic kisses of pleasure circle
your ebony treasure
like a tongue on the tip of a wine glass.
You See,
I'm the number 1 contender.
And with every "thrust" of this love...
I'm plottin' your surrender.
Your man... Oh yeah,
Tell'em now he's got something to worry about.
Why don't you get a little closer,
so both you and these lights... can get turned out.
Ecstasy in privacy, tranquility with
security, are all the qualities,
You can find with in... Never mind.
You see,
I'm the number 1 contender.
And with every "thrust" of this love...I'm
plottin' your surrender.
Get ready for the main event...

All of a sudden Rique's phone rang and it startled him! He stopped writing because he knew it had to be her, Shyla, the one girl he loved but wishes he could leave alone. "Hey you," Rique answered the phone enthusiastically.

"Hey, whats up?" Shyla said in her normal cheerful tone.

"Nothing. Are we still getting together this Friday so I can knock the bottom out that pussy?" Rique smiled to himself.

"You are so nasty, stop talking like that. But yeah, give me a call to tell me where and when you want to hook up." Shyla never showed her feelings, but Rique knew she was crazy about him too. Only he could even think of saying something like that to her and she seriously entertain it.

"I will definitely let you know Lil Thang. You still my Lil Thang?" Rique inquired.

"Yeah, I am. Why are you being so silly today?" Shyla seemed annoyed.

"I'm not being silly, I miss you. Is that ok?"

"Yeah, but you just saw me last week."

"Oh alright, I guess that means we're not on the same page. That's cool." Rique was a little hurt, but Shyla always appeared to be somewhat of a cold person to him. He tried to be understanding because he knew that she had a lot of hurt in her past and present. He often had to remind himself that she had a husband so he could put the brakes on his feelings as well.

Shyla always served as a huge inspiration for Rique's poetry, both good and bad. Love always came with a certain amount of pain for Rique because underneath all the Thicke Rique hoopla, he was very sensitive. Shyla knew that but never realized how much her little smart statements actually bothered him. Rique put his feelings in his work, so he resumed writing immediately after his conversation with Shyla, but with a major change of tone:

Diary Of A 12 Inch Brotha!

Entry #104: Fuck Buddies...

Yeah, but only because we're "Fucking Buddies"
But I stopped fuckin' you,
the day you reached up and hugged me.
As I came...
you rubbed me and said that you loved me.
You Liar!
You knew it would only increase the fire,
Amplify my desire,
and give me everything I needed to take you higher.
Thanks for the help...
But now I'm yelling help! Drowning in ecstasy,
loosely translated....
That's your wet pussy, plus me,
Which equals death on the seven seas!
Ooh Wee!
So baby sing to me,
do that thing you do to me...
With your tongue, sprung
We laugh as if we're just having fun?
And not passion filled nights,
sex outside illuminated by headlights,
Poetry with back shots, and you kissing on my open mic.
Oh, do you sympathize with this black man's plight?
You might, soon as you realize...
That I wish we could do this, every single night.

"Alright enough of that," Rique shook his head, "One day Im gonna write a book about all this shit. I should call it Dick Tales or better yet The Dick Chronicles!" Rique laughed to himself, "Sh-h-h-it, Zane might sue my ass if I swagger jacked her like that."

61

"I got it... Lifestyle of a 12 Inch Brotha! Nah, Diary of a 12... ah, never mind, what kind of person would want to read something like that anyway?" Rique smiled as he got his things together and left the hotel.

"Let me call that crazy ass sister of mine and see what's up with her today," Rique said to himself while driving home.

Ring, Ring, Ring.

"Hello?" Blaque' answered without her normal bravado or sarcasm. She sounded as if she had something on her mind.

"What's up big head? What's the deal for today? We got a meeting or something?" Rique acted like he didn't notice her tone.

"Nah, I'm over Melanie's house trying to calm her down. Last night when she dropped me off at the club, some dude started following her from the parking lot. She said he sped off when she pulled into 7 eleven where the cops were."

"Could she see his face? Can she describe him or the car at least?" Rique asked.

"No, she said it was too dark but the car looked like a funny blue-ish purple color. She's not even sure if the driver was male or female. It was probably one of them crazy ass dudes from the female show earlier though, thinking she was one of the dancers just getting off or something. I don't know." Blaque' tried to make light of the situation for Melanie's sake.

"Yeah, we need to get some parking lot security or something. Shit is getting crazy. Tell her don't worry about it too much though, it was probably an isolated incident," Rique reassured Blaque'.

"I got her, she'll be okay. I told her that she needs to get ready for the celebrity lifestyle. She married a baller. A horny little man outside of a strip club is the least of her worries. She's gonna have to deal with them female groupies all over her man... especially them white girls and dem Tila Tequilla lookin' hoes!" Blaque' smiled and put her arm around Melanie as she swayed back and forth.

"A'ight then, I'll hit you up later. Got some plans to make, word is bond!" Rique giggled mischievously.

"What the fuck does that mean? Word is bond... word is bond, why do you say that all the time? Yuck, and I hope those plans don't involve either one of them needy ass hoes of yours. Get some new meat for cryin out loud! I thought them chicks were one-nighters at best."

"What? I'm not talking to you about them anyway. So mind your business and stay out of grown folks affairs." Rique was annoyed but still said spoke jokingly.

"Speaking of affairs... it must be that trife life married chick of yours then. You been messing with that hoe on and off for like two years. A real loser if you ask me. I keep saying, why give it away for free when you can make money off of it?" Blaque' knew that would piss Rique off so she kept repeating, "Get money pimp, get money!"

"Shut the hell up Blaque'! You always gotta start..." Rique hung the phone up on her and texted Shyla to see if she could get with him that evening. Shyla texted him back and said that she could meet at Edens Lounge near downtown Baltimore around six o'clock for drinks or whatever.

"I'm looking forward to the whatever part. That's what's up!" Rique took a shower then checked out of the hotel and went to his condo in Cecil County, Maryland.

Rique's dwelling was an extension of him. It was decorated with lots of earth tones, live plants, and natural light. He was at peace in his home and rarely brought girls there, which is the reason why he made it a point to protect it. Rique bought a four thousand dollar, reinforced door that had several deadbolts in it. A hustler Rique knew told him about the door, but of course he was using it to keep the police out. To Rique home was where he laid his head to think and relax, so it was like protecting his mind.

While working out, Rique was planning to bring Shyla to his place after they left Eden's Lounge. He had brought her there many times before but that night was different because he was in the mood to play some games. Rique wanted to cook for her, bathe her, and massage her into the sex tonight. Shyla had that special thing that made him want to spoil her.

Sure she was cheating on her husband with him, but it never felt that way to Rique. In his eyes, Shyla was married to the wrong man, and he was going to prove it to her. Rique believed her to be his soul mate, who he was tailor fit to handle her pain. Her neediness was like his own, so he understood that she was hard on the outside but soft in the middle.

After cleaning his condo and taking a shower Rique began to set the scene for a sexy evening with Shyla. Unlit, scented candles were strategically placed, her favorite champagne sat on the edge of the jacuzzi, and flavored, heating massage oil all awaited Shyla's arrival.

Before Rique left for downtown Baltimore, he laid a trail of red and pink rose pedals from the door to the bathroom and bed. When he exited the condo Rique began to laugh and went into a poetic freestyle, "I'm going to eat that pussy... until her clit caves in. Flick my tongue so well that I become her favorite sin. I'm gonna bend her over the dresser... then bless her. Pull her hair until the underwear she wears... gets a little wetter. I'm no half stepper... Ricky the magnificent, tongue kiss the clit so well she writin dear John letters!"

When Rique arrived downtown there was no parking. He decided to circle the block a few times until he grew frustrated and finally called Shyla's cell phone. She didn't pick up immediately, so he sent a text message and called right back.

"Hello?" Shyla answered over the noise.

"Hey, Lil Bits. I'm outside in my car because I can't find any parking. I'm gonna pull up front in about 2 minutes. Meet me there."

"Okay, I'll be right out sexy," Shyla replied.

Shyla grabbed her last glass of Moscatto wine and downed it before placing a fifty on the bar and leaving. As usual, Edens was a meat market. There were guys touching her arm and saying wack lines trying to get some attention. Shyla ignored them, knowing that she had some good dick waiting for her out front.

A little tipsy from numerous glasses of wine, Shyla almost tripped as she got into Rique's car. As usual, she was looking good; lip gloss, tight short skirt, and heels with legs that wouldn't quit. However, it made Rique angry that she got tipsy around all the men in the lounge.

"You alright?" Rique asked sarcastically.

"Yeah, I'm cool. Just a few glasses of wine. You know how we do," replied Shyla playfully.

"No, I don't know how we do? How is that.. stumblin and lookin' like a fool? Why you gotta get like that every time we get up? Come on, it's been like two years of bull-shittin. " Rique pulled off shaking his head from side to side.

"Damn, you're starting to sound like that religious, freak husband of mine... killin my little buzz and shit. I didn't even get a hug or nothing before you started chastising me," Shyla said jokingly because she kind of liked the fact that Rique cared as much as he did. It made her feel in control.

"Shyla, stop playing with me. You know what I'm talking about. I hope you parked in a good spot because we're going back to my place."

"I'm sorry baby. We can go anywhere you want. It's alright with me. I'll make it up to you when we get there," Shyla smiled mischievously.

Rique felt that Shyla didn't take him seriously, even after two years. She was obviously comfortable with just fucking him on and off and loved the attention he gave her. In street terms, Rique was caught up, meaning he was serious about a situation that he knew he shouldn't be. Though Shyla complained about her husband being too religious and never spending any time with her, she still appeared to be comfortable with her situation as long as she had an outlet.

Shyla could tell Rique was upset with her so she placed her hand on his lap and rubbed the inside of his thigh as he drove. This made Rique grow instantly hard because he's always been infatuated with Shyla, so he reached over and began to lightly rub her pussy under her skirt. As he pulled into his condo's parking lot, both of them could not keep their hands off each other. Rique closely followed her up the stairs, pressing his dick against her ass and caressing her hips.

"Umm, wait until I get you in there boy," Shyla said as she licked her lips while Rique pressed her against his front door to open it.

"Tonight is gonna be special," stated Rique when he pushed the door open to reveal a dimly lit condo, soft music, and rose pedals.

Shyla smiled and chuckled to herself, "Why are you doing this to me?" she whined. "The sex better be off the hook tonight with all this going on."

Rique paused for a minute because that wasn't the response he was looking for. He closed the door and walked Shyla to his bedroom where he had a robe waiting.

"Wow, this is nice. What do you want me to do?" she asked.

"Take off your clothes and sit them on the chair." Rique left the room as Shyla began to get undressed. He went to the kitchen to get his whip cream, honey, strawberries, two champagne glasses and a bucket of ice. Rique prepared the bathroom by lighting the scented candles, placing the champagne in the bucket of ice and setting the two glasses at the edge of the tub. He then dimmed the lights in the bathroom and started the jacuzzi.

"Baby, hurry up... I'm ready," whined Shyla in a baby voice.

Rique didn't reply, he entered the room with the strawberries and whipped cream while Shyla stood near the bed striking a pose totally nude.

"Whipped cream and strawberries? So typical, but nice... I'm only kidding," said Shyla.

Rique still didn't reply because he was determined not to let her trivialize the mood. He sat everything down, lifted Shyla up in his arms, and took her to the bathroom. Rique passionately kissed Shyla, as he carried her and gently laid her in the water of the jacuzzi.

"Ooh, this feels so good. Baby please get in. I want that dick so badly right now it's a shame," begged Shyla.

"You gotta wait and get with the mood I'm trying to set nasty. There is so much more so be patient, sit back, and enjoy," softly whispered Rique.

He popped the cork on the champagne and poured two glasses. Rique took his clothes all off and his dick hung like a thick juicy piece of steak for Shyla to enjoy. Every time they had sex, for some strange reason, Shyla would always crave meat. Rique handed her one of the glasses of champagne while he sipped his and slowly got into the Jacuzzi.

"To us, spending quality time together and loving every bit of it. I love you Shy-Shy." Rique waited for a response but there was none. Shyla smiled and took her whole glass of champagne to the head. Rique poured her another glass immediately, slid behind her, and began to rub her pussy underwater. While Shyla held her glass up, her head swayed from side to side, and Rique broke into a poetic freestyle inspired by her.

"Mmm, baby I wonder… how many men have been lost at sea? And will I be taken under by the current of you and me? If so… then Gilligan I'll be. So just send me to school in your whirlpool, take a deep breath, and count to three. Anxiously I'll go down to take Neptune's crown because I'm no chicken of the sea. Please… most men need oxygen to breathe, but soon you'll find that their tanks are on empty, when they won't help the little man in the boat every time he's truly lost at sea!

But hold on…I'm coming with abilities you won't believe; with the agility of Achilles and the power of Zeus to tame the high seas. Now sit up on your knees, over top of me. My tongue is now in your rain forest, wielding through the trees. Put your hands on the wall and move. Now I can feel your legs shakin. In a minute you can turn and flip, let your lips embrace my tip, and get the cool whip I've been savin!"

Shyla's head dropped back onto Rique's shoulder. She sat the glass on the side and panted as she began to fuck his fingers underwater. Rique's dick was rock hard and pressed against her back. Things were getting too hot in the water, so Rique stood up and sat Shyla on the side of the jacuzzi. She reached out and started circling the head of his dick before Rique pulled back and grabbed two terry cloth robes.

"Let's go to the bedroom," Rique ordered.

Wrapped in the robe, Rique carried Shyla to the bedroom and laid her on the bed. He pulled some silk scarves out of the top drawer of his nightstand. Shyla saw them and looked a little worried.

"What are you gonna do with those baby?" Shyla questioned.

"Shut up and gimmie your hands. You're a big girl right?" Rique spoke forcibly because he knew it turned her on when done at the right moment.

Shyla loved when he took control, so she was eager to comply. Rique tied her wrist and blindfolded her with the scarves. He opened her robe as she laid on the bed waiting for his next move.

"Relax baby, I need you to totally trust me right now. Do you trust me?" Rique whispered seductively.

"Yeah baby," she murmured.

Rique slowly kissed every part of her body, while he pulled massage oil and a big white feather out of his night stand. He then lightly traced the feather across her breast and stomach as he kissed around her pussy and circled her clit. Shyla jerked periodically and seductively moved her body in a wave like motion. Rique sat the feather aside then poured massage oil in his hand. He warmed it by cupping his hands and breathing in them, then he began to rub it all over her highly aroused breast.

Shyla's nipples were already hard, so Rique licked and sucked on them thru the massage oil to intensify her feeling. Shyla began to grind the air as Rique slowly kissed back down to her pussy.

"Stop right there. Baby please talk, do a poem, or something while you're eating my pussy," Shyla pleaded. "Talk to me please, it turns me on so much!"

Being blindfolded heightened her other senses and amplified the feeling beyond her imagination. Rique had her mind right where he wanted it, so he began to passionately freestyle a poem while he slowly ate her pussy.

"Let's get back to the basics. Lick! Like basically what a man is supposed to be. Then multiple him by three. Lick! Yea, that's me. Three sets of hands all over your body. Late night, lights out, candles with just me and your body. Lick! Who am I? Nobody important. Lick! Cuz tonight, it's all about you and everything we do.

Now you shut up and enjoy this blindfold. Lick! I got the massage oil prepared for you. Take off your clothes, now you're both mentally & physically exposed. Lick!

You say; Rique it's cold! No, that's ice." Rique paused to put the ice in his mouth from the champagne ice bucket. Lick!"

"Yes, I said ice and guess where it goes? Lick, Lick! As I massage your front, yes, your breast and chest, match the motion of my hands. Can I be your man? Lick! Well for tonight at least... My questions whispered softly as I kiss the crease... Lick! of your chest, between your breast. Oh Yes! So what's next? Lick! Poetry in circles, around your left nipple... Lick! The tongue that speaks, seeks to take you to your peak. Which we both know isn't that simple. Lick! As I kiss and lick to deliver the sweetest bliss, tell me if there's any part of your body I miss. Lick!

I wanna do it right, so that every night when I hold you tight, it feels like our last night... together. Lick! I never want to take you for granted. Granted, these are the things I say before I take on the little man in the boat, single handed. Lick! You're blind folded, remember! Hard as hell, I swell. Can your leg feel my member? Lick!

Ice cubes make my tongue cold as December, so I say my grace before I start to taste as if it were the 25th of November, Thanksgiving. Lick, Lick! Your legs can drape these broad shoulders, before I get my filling. Lick! So I can implore slow to rapid sensual drilling. Appealing? Lick! You're blind folded, remember? So stop reaching for the ceiling. Lick...Lick...Lick!"

Rique continued eating Shyla's pussy until she began to shake, jerk and cum. She tried to grab his head at climax, but he pulled back.

"Don't stop, what the fuck?" Shyla was about to get angry but Rique came up with the hardest dick she's felt in years.

"Oh shit, right their baby," Shyla screeched.

"I need to get a condom," suggested Rique.

"Fuck that, don't stop! Don't you fuckin' stop, to the left...right there! Ooh yes, right there baby!" Shyla barked orders while continually breathing heavy and positioning Rique's dick to just the right location.

Rique began feeling the sensation of heat in his balls because he too was about to cum. All the intimacy and excitement had them both caught up. Shyla grabbed Rique's back and started humping frantically upward on his dick as she started to cum. Instantly; Rique started digging his twelve inches deep in Shyla until she let out a moan and started tapping his back.

"You a big girl, you can take it," Rique whispered in response to her tapping.

"Oh baby, that's too dee-p!" Shyla yelled, but it was too late. Rique had already cupped her shoulders, arched his back, and started grinding in big circles deep inside until he felt like his dick was going to explode in her pussy. Caught in the moment, both Rique and Shyla came at the same time without thinking about anything.

"Did you pull out in time?" Shyla asked out of breath.

"Yeah. Damn, you act like I'm trying to get you pregnant or something," Rique was annoyed.

They started arguing immediately after having sex and Shyla didn't understand why. Rique was growing more sensitive than usual all of a sudden which wasn't a good sign to her. She had been in this type of situation before so she knew all the signs.

"As usual, you always miss the point. That was great, so I'm definitely not gonna let an argument ruin it. I can get that at home from my proverb quoting husband so spare me the drama right now."

"I don't like the way you act sometimes. I don't feel like you take me serious. Anyway, why don't you come to any of my shows?" Rique asked sternly.

"Oh boy please, here we go again. Let's not forget that I met you at my girlfriend's bachelorette party when I thought you were just a Dee-jay. I had no idea you got naked too. It's just not my thing; we've been over this before."

"Got naked too? What's that supposed to mean? It's like you look down on me or something. I thought that maybe you would come to the show we're having tonight and support me," Rique probed.

"Why are you trying to argue with me? You already know the answer! Look, live your life the way you want; I'm not a part of that side of it. I'm ready to go now Rique."

Shyla gathered her things and went into the bathroom. While she was in the bathroom, Rique sat at the edge of the bed and left a message on his sister's voicemail that he would not be working tonight.

"Shy, Shy!" Rique called to Shyla while she was still in the bathroom.

Shyla opened the door half dressed and asked, "Yes?"

"Why don't we chill and go check out this brotha that's speaking tonight at Life Fellowship Christian church. I hear he's really good and tonight he's gonna be talking about relationships."

"What? How you go from strip club to church is mind boggling to me. Hell no! You know my husband is a religious freak; I don't want to see another church. Plus, what kind of church is holding service this late on a week night?"

"I said there was a special speaker tonight, so there's a special service. Helping people is a seven day a week job Shyla," Rique said sarcastically.

"Well, some people need more help than others because some people obviously are not living in reality. Don't you have to go to work anyway?"

"Just because you're married doesn't mean I shouldn't care about your well being. I do live in reality; the one I make, not the one that's given to me. Try it sometime; you might be happy one day. Never mind, forget it. I'll go by myself, as usual."

Rique dismissed Shyla as she slammed the bathroom door and prepared to be driven back to her car. After seeing how she acted, Rique decided to call Melanie's cell to see if she'd go with him to hear the speaker at the church. Melanie liked doing things like that and she was usually home if not with Blaque' because Dalvin was so frequently out of town with his team or on business.

"Hey Mel, its Rique. They're having a speaker at the Christian Center tonight. Are you trying to go?"

Chapter V:
Pimpstress

"What?" Blaque' listened to her brother's message from her voicemail. "I know this motherfucker ain't gonna miss another night! This has got to stop; I'm callin him back right now!"

Blaque' attempted to call Rique but his phone was off and it kept going straight to voicemail, "Yo, where the fuck are you? This is a business; you can't just leave everyone hanging like that. Don't cut off your phone and disappear when you supposed to be my partner. What kind of shit is that? Call me when you fuckin' find the time!"

"Psst, psst, Mistress!" The dancer Donnie Cockerin was trying to get her attention.

Blaque' hung up the phone, "Boy, what do you want? Didn't you see that I was on the phone?"

"I'm sorry, but I wanted to let you know that we got two a piece already."

"Already, but it's only nine o'clock?" Blaque' laughed and continued, "These hoes are off the hook, buying dick... at least something's going right. Well, ya'll know what to do, why are you telling me?"

"Cuz I heard that Officer Friendly dude tell his girls to meet him out back in his van again."

"So this motherfucker is not tryin' to pay me, huh? Alright, I got his number. Let him do his thing so that we don't draw any attention from the other dancers. Take your girls to the spot and tell John the Titan to cover for you. I'll deal with Officer Friendly when the time is right."

Blaque' went to the Dee-jay booth to emcee and put on the mix CD that Rique prepared in the event of his absence. While in the booth, she could see the hoards of women with Thicke Rique The Poet shirts on. Blaque' thought about why Rique said he changed his name for Rique da Ruler to Rique the poet. He thought that the new name would appeal to a broader base of women and he was right.

Blaque' saw the two girls that Donnie had told her about earlier leaving the club after being huddled up with Officer Friendly. She then watched him slowly slip out the side door himself. Blaque' smiled and went to get her purse from the back locker.

"This dude really thinks that shit is sweet around here. He's gonna use my clientele, my stage, and my place to get his fuck on and not pay me my cut? Oh, he's got it twisted!"

Blaque' went out the back door of the club to Officer Friendly's van. She approached it slowly from the side to see if she could hear anything. As she got closer, the van started to move and she could overhear two voices moaning.

"That's it. Fuck her good, make my home girl cum. Tell the officer you sorry Destiny. Tell him you sorry for being a bad girl," said the woman's best friend.

"Why are you fucking me in this van? You know that's illegal right? You're a bad girl? I'm gonna spank your ass while you take this night stick. I should put your ass in jail. Would you like that?" said Officer Friendly to Destiny.

The van started to bounce harder and harder. Blaque' wanted to make sure he was good and deep in that pussy before she did anything.

"Save me some Officer Friendly," said the other female voice.

The van bounced increasingly faster and the women's voices elevated to high pitched squeals before Blaque' tried the rear door handle and flung it open.

"Where the hell is my money motherfucker?" Blaque' yelled.

Both of the women and Officer Friendly almost jumped through the roof they were so scared. One woman was kneeling doggy-style with Friendly behind her ass out, while the other was riding his back topless watching them fuck.

"Bitch, you better close that fuckin' door! Don't bust up in my shit like that. This is my van... my property," Friendly shouted angrily.

Blaque' looked on both sides of her then said, "Bitch? Not yet, but I will be if you don't kick me my doe right now. A hundred fifty for miss doggy-style right here, a hundred fifty for back rider, and fifty for missing time on the floor while your trifling ass was doing this shit. That's three fiddy... kick out my gwop!"

"You crazy, I ain't giving you shit! Shut my fuckin' door before I get up from here," threatened Friendly.

"Wrong answer.... Wrong fucking answer! I will get my money one way or another and you will be naked on that floor tonight like you supposed to be," said Blaque' calmly as she shut the door and walked away.

The women were so scared of her that they hurried to pay Officer Friendly so Blaque' wouldn't come after them, then ran to their car and sped off. One of them left their purse behind and didn't even realize it. Friendly threw it in the front seat, put on half of his clothes and boldly went back into the club. When he got backstage, he saw Blaque' staring at him and smiling. He shrugged her off and packed his things to leave.

"I quit bi-aoch," Friendly said as he walked by her to exit the building.

Blaque' looked at him and said out loud to herself, "Not yet, I'm not a bitch yet."

As Officer Friendly walked through the parking, lot he could see that someone was standing near his van. He assumed it was one of the girls coming to get her purse, but when he got closer he could see that it wasn't. At that moment, he was struck on the back of the head with a blunt object. He wasn't unconscious, but he still fell to the ground. Friendly looked up and saw two guns pointed at him with two masked men peeking out from behind the barrels.

"Gimmie everything you got. Don't turn this shit into a homicide!" One of the men whispered in a hostile tone.

"Aw man, what's this all about..." Friendly tried to speak but his question was cut short by numerous kicks to the side and chest from both assailants.

"Bitch, I said kick that gwop and shut the fuck up! Say one more word and we're gonna make that shirt polka dot!"

"Alright, calm down man... damn," shouted Officer Friendly before nervously complying with their demands. He gave them his wallet with about seven hundred and fifty dollars out of his pockets. They made him get up and take off all of his clothes behind the dumpster on the side of the club. One robber went to get the car while the other walked him up to the side door of the club and said, "I'm gonna count to three, and if you are not in that door by then I'm gonna bust your ass, straight up. One..."

Diary Of A 12 Inch Brotha!

The other robber fired a shot in the air out of the window on the other side of the car. Officer Friendly took off running into the club, across the dance floor, and back out the rear door. Everyone in the club heard the shot but wasn't sure what it was because Blaque' had turned the music up so loud in the Dee-jay booth. Most of the women thought it was a part of the show however, and started throwing money at Officer Friendly as he ran across the floor.

Now paranoid, Friendly waited behind the club for a while to make sure the coast was clear. He looked all around then darted to his van where he found his window busted on the passenger side. He opened the driver's door, still naked, and got a spare set of keys out of a secret compartment under his chair. As he started the van he noticed that his wallet was on the passenger seat with all of his money in it except exactly three hundred and fifty dollars. It sent a message he got clearly and only confirmed what he already knew. Officer Friendly backed his van up and screeched out of the parking lot at top speed.

Blaque''s cell phone rang while she was backstage looking out of the window and laughing hysterically. She answered the phone and said, "What happened to the tough guy? Okay, now I am the bitch he called me." Blaque' thanked her cousins and told them to keep the money because they had exceeded her expectations on this one.

Later that evening after the show, Blaque' had a meeting with all the dancers while they were getting dressed. She entered the room quietly, slowly walking back and forth. The dancers stopped their personal conversations and waited for Blaque' to address them.

"Okay guys, I think that we all can agree that this has been one crazy night. I'd like to thank everyone that stepped up in the absence of my brother. I know his attendance has been irregular at best."

"Is he alright?" One dancer asked.

"Oh he's fine...just a little beside himself, that's all. I plan on having a sit down with him and getting things back on track. Which brings me to Officer Friendly; he will no longer be a part of this dance troop," Blaque' said sternly.

"You know I got ya back Blaque'! Plus, I know another dude name Chocolate that would be perfect to replace him," Donnie Cockerin blurted out eagerly.

"Thank you Donnie. Some of you may have heard rumors about me... both good and bad. Some of them are true and some of them are not, but one thing is for sure; if you want to make money, you are in the right place.

I am promoting Donnie Cockerin to head dancer, so if you boys need any help or just want to know how to get ahead in this business... see him. All percentage monies and scheduling will go through him from now on. Everyone, please settle your tab at the bar before you leave. Thank you. Donnie, I need to see you in my office."

Blaque' went back to the small office Tony made for her in the back of the club. While she waited for Donnie and Tony to come in with the night's totals, she decided to call Rique again. He didn't answer the phone so she decided to leave him a message.

"Alright Rique, this shit is getting ridiculous. You haven't even called back from earlier. Don't expect to get paid if I'm doing all the work. This business needs you for a reason and everyone expects you to be here. I had to cut... oops, I mean fire Officer Friendly tonight. Shit is really getting out of hand. Call me when you get this."

Tony and Donnie came in shortly after Blaque' left her message for Rique. They both had money bags and ledger cards with them. Blaque' pulled out her laptop and began to plug in the numbers from the nights take.

"Alright guys, here it goes in a nut shell. We did well tonight, but we do much better when my brother's here. I'll take care of him, but we need to clearly define our responsibilities so that we can handle the apparent growth we are having."

"Cool, I'm with that Blaque', but I don't think that we are going to be able to hide and grow the male prostitution from your brother much longer. The women are getting more and more aggressive. Some even tried to pay me" said Tony, the club owner."

"You are too funny Tony, but stop calling them male prostitutes. We use the term Sexcorts. That's why I said let's sit down and get it more organized. Tony, you need to have two sets of bouncers. One set that knows what's going on and others that don't. The ones that know, should be on the inside protecting all the back bedroom activities for the Sexcorts. The ones that don't, should be on the front door and outside patrolling the parking lot. They serve as protection because they don't know anything and will give us early warnings of the police. Like tonight for instance, the police came because a shot was fired, but we looked like the victims," Blaque' explained with pinpoint precision.

"Sounds good, and I'll make one of the guys that's down with us the head of the guys that don't know anything," Tony added.

"Great idea, we'll work out the kinks as we go. Donnie, you are the point man. You screen the dancers after they've been here for a while to see if they have the mentality to be Sexcorts, some will... some won't. You'll also screen the clientele for new customers and facilitate our regulars, so like Rique; you'll only dance in the finale.

You guys take care of your areas and I will oversee everything. I will be the strong arm when we need one for snitches. Make me the bad guy if you get back talk from anybody. Whether it's a dancer, club employee, or customer, I will take care of them... I will take care of them personally," Blaque' grabbed her purse and squeezed it to reveal a gun shaped object, "or through remote means like my cousins did tonight."

"Sounds good Blaque', except for the fact that I'm going to have to give up one third of my bar now and add more security out of my pocket," stated Tony.

"First things first, start paying your staff weekly not this nightly bullshit. That means bartenders, bouncers, and waitresses. This place has to appear more legit. In order to do that, we have to function more legitimately... no more under the table employees paid in cash. This will give us cover and flexibility when we tally up the bar, door, dancer percentages, and Sexcort money. All your bills will be paid before anyone gets paid.

I may get part of the bar and door, but you will now get a part of dancer percentages and Sexcort earnings which will prove to be more lucrative. The immediate goal is to get enough regular customers and serious Sexcorts so that we can separate the two businesses and only use the club to recruit new people. The money will be flowing in if we follow the plan and obtain the goal. Do you have any more questions?"

"Yeah, as a matter of fact I do have two major questions. How does your brother feel about our new partnership and is he gonna be a Sexcort or not because that's where the real money is," Tony and Donnie agreed in unison.

"Like I told ya'll before, Rique is going thru a little bit right now. I'm gonna take care of him and get his mind where it needs to be. Is that it?"

The two of them nodded yes while Blaque' dispersed the money and ended the meeting. Her cousins waited in their other car outside the club and followed her home. At least one of them did this every night and no one knew about it, not even Rique. It was her cousins' full time job to trail her and watch her back all the time. They were never far away during those hours anyway because she paid them well to be her X-factor and third eye.

Blaque' believed in covering all her bases, just in case something went wrong. That's why she was now grooming Donnie to take Rique's position, just in case he continued to miss shows or wasn't down with her Sexcort idea. She even had a plan ready if Donnie or Tony turned snitch... an unfortunate robbery homicide. That's the way it was with her. If you knew something that could potentially harm her, there was already a plan in place for your demise if needed.

When Blaque' arrived home, she called Melanie, as she did every night to let her know that she had made it in safely. "Hey girl, I'm finally home. What are you doin up? I expected the answering machine to pick up."

"Girl, I can't even sleep. I went to see a speaker down at the church. He was dynamic; it really made me think about my life and priorities. You should have been there."

"You know that's not my thing girl, but I'm glad you had a good time. Who'd you go with?"

Melanie didn't want to lie to Blaque' but she also promised Rique that she wouldn't tell Blaque' where he was so she paused then said, "A friend."

"A friend? What you mean a friend? I know you are not creepin out on Dalvin with your pregnant ass," Blaque' shouted.

Melanie laughed at her before saying, "Of course not silly, you said it... I'm pregnant, so how is that gonna happen? You don't need to know errthang about my life; I don't know everything about yours? Exactly like I said... I went with a friend."

"Oh alright, I was about to say everybody must be going crazy today! Let me tell you what happened at the club. Well for one thing, Mr. Thicke Head Rique, the bullshit poet, didn't show up again! This asshole leaves me a message saying that he won't be in. I called him back, and he didn't even have the balls to answer the phone.

Then, I had to put this dancer in his place tonight. He didn't want to perform, started talking all this testosterone driven mess, and even called me a bitch like three times! I said ok, I got your bitch right here. I sure called Marcus and them to handle that ass. Girl, by the time they got finished with him, that fool was running all around the club naked and screaming like a bitch himself!" Blaque' laughed hysterically thinking about Officer Friendly.

"Oh my god, no you didn't Bee. You better be careful. People take things personally sometimes. Plus, you know Marcus and them take things too far in certain situations. They are not wrapped too tight."

"Yeah I know girl, and I did have a feeling like someone was following me like a month or two ago," remarked Blaque'.

"What? It's funny you would say that because I told my mystery friend the exact same thing. I've been feeling that way for a while now; like somebody is watching me. I thought I was being paranoid because I was pregnant. What do you think?" Melanie asked insecurely.

"I think we should get off this phone, stop acting like we in the movie Scream, and go to bed. This is silly, and I am not going to sit up worrying about it and neither should you."

"You're right; I'm going to bed too. Goodnight Bee, holler at me tomorrow."

"Goodnight Melly Mel!"

Chapter VI:
The Doc 2

Early the next morning Blaque' went to her appointment with Doctor Joyce. She enjoyed mentally sparring with the doctor because she took pleasure in seeing if she could extract information without revealing anything too major about herself.

"Hey Doc, how ya doin?" Blaque' walked into the office and sat in her usual chair. Doctor Joyce sat still and acknowledged her with only a nod. She made note that Blaque' assumed a defensive position right from the beginning by folding her arms. There were a number of possible reasons she would do this, but Dr. Joyce believed the only real reason was that Blaque' saw her as some type of an adversary.

"Dang Doc, I just sat in the chair and you're writing already. What's up with that?" Blaque' questioned.

"Does it make you nervous when I write? What do you think I'm writing?" Dr. Joyce questioned Blaque' back. She was not going to let her turn the session into an argument or challenge as she often liked to do.

"Nah, it doesn't make me nervous because I don't know what you're writing. That's why I asked."

"It may make you nervous if you think the only time I write is when there's something wrong. Let me make this clear; there are no right or wrong answers in this office. I'm here to help you understand what you don't know about yourself."

Dr. Joyce didn't ask her a question to begin the session because she wanted to see where Blaque' was going to steer the conversation. There was a silence in the room for a moment that was symbolic of a mental stand-off between the two women. Finally, Blaque' decided to break the silence by beginning with a question concerning her brother.

"Doc, do you think it would be wrong of me to offer my brother a buy out?"

"A buyout? How did it feel for you to ask me that question? By the look on your face I think you already know the answer," stated Dr. Joyce with apprehension.

"Okay, maybe I do know but I need to know why? Why would it be wrong if he seems to have lost interest? He's missing shows and is unwilling to expand the business."

"At last, the real reason you want him gone. He's unwilling to expand the business in the way you would like, huh?"

"So what's the answer Doc?" asked Blaque'.

"Did you hear my question? How are you planning to expand the business and how do you know he won't want to?"

"You don't need to know all that to answer my damn question," defiantly responded Blaque'.

"I'm sorry; I didn't know you practiced psychiatry too Blaque'. I ask questions to get to the root of an issue, so I may need to know more details to answer properly. Is that okay with you?"

Dr. Joyce leaned back in her chair, jotted down some notes, and attempted to answer the question even though she knew there was more to the story.

"Well Blaque', I believe that your brother would see it as wrong because you want to buy him out for selfish reasons. He obviously isn't serving your purpose, so now you want more control. In other words, if he was your employee, you would fire him right now."

Blaque' put her finger to her chin, nodded her head, and said, "You're good... I mean really good. That's the only reason I continue to come. You should change the sign on the door from psychiatrist to bad ass psychic chick."

"Thank you Blaque'... I think. On the surface it seemed that your world revolved around your job. However, after a closer look, I can see that it doesn't. It revolves around attaining the benefits that your job brings you, like money and power. You have no love for what you do, that's a big problem."

"Money and power right? Well, isn't that what everybody wants from their job? I mean really... isn't that why you do what you do?"

"No, I do what I do because I love to help people and give them advice. If you offered me another job making more money doing something else, I would have to say no. I didn't choose a job; I chose a career when I decided to practice psychiatry."

"In that case, there is an aspect of my job that I do love and would never stop," replied Blaque' as she smiled sadistically.

"Oh really, what aspect would that be?" Dr. Joyce was intrigued both professionally and personally by Blaque''s statement.

"Never mind Doc, you aren't ready for that. Besides, that's one part of me I'm not willing to share. I don't need any help in that department, trust me. However, we are going to have to cut this short for today because I have some major errands to run."

"Blaque', we need to increase the sessions so they can be more beneficial to you. At this point, I feel that your issues need more attention. The next time we meet, I would like you to bring a sample of your brother's writing."

Dr. Joyce's curiosity was starting to get the best of her; she felt a need to know more about Blaque''s life beyond a professional interest. A personal connection had formed between the two women from their many clashes of personalities, and she didn't fully understand it.

"Not gonna happen Doc. That boy only writes in his little diary book, and he guards it with his life. Plus, more frequent sessions would be too much money and time. I'm ready to shine and push life to the limit. I can't be stuck up in here with you all the time!"

"Since it's my recommendation, I would work with you on the fees. As far as the time goes... it's what's needed for me to really help you."

Blaque' paused for a moment, looked at Dr. Joyce, and said, "Nah, I'm good. I gotta go Doc."

"Okay, if that's how you feel, but I really do need to see more of you," Dr. Joyce insisted.

Blaque' shrugged her shoulders as she grabbed her purse and exited the office. She appreciated Dr. Joyce's interest, but didn't want her too close for comfort. The last thing Blaque' wanted was someone to make her second guess what she was doing while she was finally making some progress. She considered stopping the sessions for a while, or at least until she had built an empire.

Later that night, Blaque' went to the club early to brainstorm and organize some things. She had spoken to Melanie earlier that day about some changes she wanted to make in the club. Together she and Tony created two areas for the dancers; one for regular dancers and the other for the Sexcorts. She wanted to create a hierarchy among them in an effort to recruit more Sexcorts from the new dancers. Blaque' definitely planned on turning some men out and taking it to the next level, even down low and gay men.

Rique walked in with his bag, looked at Blaque' from across the room, and continued to walk backstage. Blaque' wasted no time going backstage to confront him.

"Well, look what the cat dragged in. Isn't that what the old people used to say? Where the hell have you been?"

Rique was silent as he unpacked his bag. He didn't even look at her. He opened his locker and hung up his jacket. Blaque' watched him ignore her and grew angrier with every second that ticked by.

"I guess you answered my question with your silence. You don't care about the business or anything that we've built together. I have to cover for you when you're not here, and it makes me look stupid when people ask me where you are and I don't know! So I'm asking you again... what's up with you?"

"I apologize Bee. I've got a lot on my mind, and I know that I'm not as focused as I should be right now. I needed some time to myself, so I went to this church and listened to a speaker they had. I called and left a message for you, did you get it?"

"Yeah, I got that funky ass message, but that didn't do me any good. I needed you to be here. You can't leave a message the same day you're supposed to show-up. What kinda shit is that? Get it together Rique. Ain't none of them hoes worth it."

"Damn, I said my fault. Why do you constantly think everything I do is about a woman? I'm trying to get my spirit right, word is bond!"

"There you go with that word is bond shit again. It is whatever you say it is little brother, but you and I know the truth. These chicks out here have your head all screwed up and now you're fucking up plain and simple. Do whatever you want on your own time, but don't miss anymore shows. Now that's word is bond!"

"What? You don't even know how to say it right," Rique laughed as he prepared his clothes for that night's performance.

As the evening went on, a line started to form in front of the The Swingin' Cable Club. Blaque' had all the bouncers and dancers on point. Tony was at his post making sure the bar was ready and the venue was tight. Rique looked as toned and ready as ever, he was backstage joking with the other guys about how he was going to introduce them. Everything looked great; the crowd, the employees, the entertainment, and the venue were all on point.

Blaque' went backstage to speak to the dancers while they were getting ready for the show. The new dancers were unsure why they were separated in the same room, so one of them asked, "What's up with the assigned lockers General Bee?"

"My name is Blaque'. Miss Blaque' if you're nasty and yes, I am the general." Blaque' was joking with them but she did it so rarely that they weren't sure she was kidding.

"You're real funny with that one. But seriously, why the locker assignments?" Rique asked.

"Well brother and all of you if you must know; it's an easy way for the club's staff to distinguish the new temp dancers from the permanent ones when they clean. No big conspiracy or nothing like that."

Donnie looked at Blaque' and smiled because he knew the real reason. Rique noticed the new closeness forming between Donnie and Blaque'. She announced that he would be taking care of certain nightly duties and reporting back to her. This disturbed Rique because they were supposed to be partners but she never even mentioned it to him.

"Guys, I want you to give it to them tonight! We have the biggest crowd we've ever had so there is a lot of money out there. Let's get it!" Blaque' wanted the guys pumped up because she saw opportunities to not only make money but to grow her business.

"Rique, there's a young lady here to see you." One of the bouncers came to the back to alert Rique that Niagara was looking for him.

"A'ight, I'll be right there," said Rique.

Blaque' rolled her eyes as Rique walked by her and said, "Remember what I told you about them hoes."

"Whatever girl, I'm a grown ass man. You should have told me about your boy and his new promotion. That's what you should have told me."

"Well, if you were here more you would have known or better yet, maybe I wouldn't have needed him. Check yourself before you wreck yourself little brother!"

"Don't start, I'm warning you Bee," said Rique.

"No, as you can see... I'm warning you," responded Blaque' sternly.

Rique looked at Blaque' with distain because it was clear to him that she valued the business more than their relationship as brother and sister. He walked to the front, where he saw Niagara in a fitted tee and black leggings with her hair pulled back into a long pony tail. She looked fine as ever but it had no affect on Rique because his mind was on building a meaningful relationship with Shyla. As a matter of fact, he wanted to distance himself from the temptation of party girls like Niagara, but it wasn't going to be easy. He could already feel Niagara pulling closer to him as he tried to get himself together mentally.

"Hey you, what are you doing here?" asked Rique.

"Well, I wanted to see you tonight and was hoping that afterwards we could chill or maybe go to an afterhours spot," Niagara suggested.

"Girl, you know I'll be crazy tired after the show. Plus, I plan on having a sit down with Blaque' on a few issues I'm having with her management style. It's not going to be pretty so I don't think you want to be around to see that."

"Alright, I understand, but I'm a little disappointed because I really wanted to spend some time tonight. You better not be trying to get rid of me so you can get with one of these chicken heads out here screaming your name," joked Niagara.

"Yeah right," said Rique.

"Alright, don't make me have to run up on a chick like… what!"

Both Rique and Niagara laughed it off, but deep down inside he felt that she was serious. Niagara leaned in and kissed Rique on the cheek before she exited from backstage. Rique dismissed his uncomfortable feelings because he had bigger things on his mind.

The show began in usual fashion, with Rique serving as the master of ceremonies and introducing each dancer. Blaque' scanned the room and saw that there wasn't an empty seat in the house. Women were standing everywhere, even blocking the fire exits. Blaque' immediately went to the front of the club to alert the bouncers and pick up the door money. Tony couldn't leave the bar area because the crowd bombarded the bartenders and servers with orders.

After he introduced the second set, Rique did his usual stroll to the bar area to get himself a drink. As much as he hated to admit it, Rique still loved the attention of the lime light. He would transform into his alter ego, a super ego called Thicke Rique Da Ruler. For the first time in his life, he could see that it wasn't just a stage name any longer. It had become a completely different personality; an extreme extension of himself that he was addicted to.

As Rique approached the bar, a woman in a slightly tight, grey business suit with a short skirt caught his eye. She was firmly packed in by the crowd, peeking out from between the arms and breast of other women sitting at the bar. When Rique ordered his drink, he smiled at her to see if he could get a positive reaction. She smiled back and blushed at the same time, so he knew everything was a go if he wanted to pursue it.

"Now I know you can't be comfortable sitting here." Rique spoke to her loudly over the music.

"No not really, but where else could I fit?" she replied.

"Aw, you're just a little old thing; you can't take up much space. I bet I can find a spot for you, if you hand me my beer when it comes."

The woman giggled and almost knocked her glass of wine over. She appeared to be taken by Rique's casual conversation. He liked flirting with her because she was classy and not aggressive like most of the women in the club.

"What's so funny?" Rique asked.

"Nothing, you're just blocking my view of the show."

"What? Aw man, now that's funny. You played me hard!" Rique put his hand over his face and couldn't stop laughing at her flirtatious dis.

The woman got up from the bar stool and handed Rique his drink before saying, "Come on playa. Keep your end of the bargain. Where are we going?"

"Oh, you are just too much miss business suit. I hope you brought some sneakers with you because you and I might have to fight after this."

Rique took her by the hand to a space cleared for VIP guests. He noticed her shape as she sat down but didn't comment because he knew it would be the wrong move.

"Okay, now you can see the show clearly. Is there anything else you would like this servant to do for you?"

"You're not a servant, you're Thicke Rique Da Ruler," she said jokingly.

"A lot of good that's doing me; you know my name but I don't know yours."

Rique smiled at the woman and slightly tilted his head in a humble manner, in an attempt to use his boy-like charm on her. Before he could get her name he noticed Niagara staring at him from the side with a scowl on her face and her hand on her hip. Rique ignored Niagara but kept her in sight while he continued with his conversation.

"So what's your name again?"

"I said Vee," she replied.

"V, as in Viagara?" Rique joked.

"No, Vee as in Doctor," she responded sarcastically.

"What? There's no V in doctor?"

Rique lost track of Niagara in the crowd as he conversed. His eyes briefly scanned the room before she popped up right beside him.

"You didn't see me over there?" Niagara asked.

"Yeah I saw you, but I was talking as you can see."

"So what's next? Are you going to send her a bottle of hypnotic too?"

Rique didn't even answer Niagara's question because to him she was acting like a complete ass. The woman turned away from their conversation and shook her head. She looked at the show for a moment but felt uncomfortable, so she got up to leave.

"Oh, you can't answer me? Maybe I'll ask her then... excuse me miss thang," Niagara questioned sarcastically. She looked the woman up and down in an attempt to intimidate her.

"What the hell are you doing Niagara? I barely even know her," Rique interrupted. He knew Niagara would cause a scene, so he had to try to accommodate her feelings at that moment.

"Barely know her huh? What the fuck ever! Why she all up in VIP, while I can barely get a two minute conversation out your ass. Fuck her!"

Blaque' saw the commotion from across the room so she began to make her way through the crowd. Rique saw her and begged Niagara to calm down because he knew it was about to get ugly. Niagara turned back towards the woman, who was scared to death at that point, and listened to her explain how she knew Rique.

"Check this out; I don't care how the fuck you know him. Just get your school teacher looking ass out of my man's face before I..." Niagara shouted with her hand in the woman's face.

"Doctor Joyce?" Blaque' interrupted.

Once she was closer to the altercation Blaque' recognized that the woman Niagara was arguing with was her psychiatrist. Dr. Joyce was so relieved to see Blaque' that she reached out to hug her. Blaque' smirked for a minute because she was totally surprised to see Dr. Joyce in a strip club. However, the moment was cut short by Niagara's attitude, as she turned back towards Rique and further addressed the issue before Blaque' grabbed her shoulder to check her ass.

"Bitch, didn't we have to kick you out one time before," shouted Blaque'.

"Bitch? Who do you think..." Niagara tried to respond.

"That's right, I said bitch. Do you want me to spell it out for you? B-I-T-C..."

"No, you ain't got to spell it for me at all boo, boo! If you see a bitch, you slap a bitch!" Niagara said defiantly.

The bouncers saw Blaque' mush Niagara in the face so they surrounded the area. Rique got between the two women and begged them to stop. He tried to calm the situation by telling the bouncers to chill for a moment because he had it under control.

Blaque' clutched her purse and responded, "You know what? You're not even worth it. You get a pass this time, but if you ever...."

When Blaque' turned to walk away, Rique and the bouncers tried to calm Niagara's bad attitude. She rolled her eyes and told the bouncers that they better not touch her or there would be hell to pay because she was nobody's joke. Then, before anyone had a chance to respond, Blaque' jumped across the men and wrapped her hand in Niagara's pony tail. She raised her purse high in the air and swung down across Niagara's face. Blaque' struck her quickly several times, as she yelled warnings of pending harm.

Diary Of A 12 Inch Brotha!

"You don't run shit around here bitch! Listen to what the fuck I tell you and get outta here while you still can. I mean it! I'm queen in this motherfucker! Don't play with me; it will be the worst mistake in your fuckin' life!"

The bouncers pried Blaque''s fingers open to release Niagara's hair, while most stayed to watch the fiasco, some people ran to exit the club. Once her pony tail was released, Niagara's lip started to bleed, and she slowly stumbled to the floor. She felt the blows of a blunt object that Blaque' was obviously holding in her purse.

Rique restrained his sister because the bouncers were too afraid of getting fired or humiliated like Officer Friendly. Niagara slowly got to her feet with the help of one bouncer, while the others started clearing everyone away. As Rique restrained Blaque', no one bothered to hold Niagara, so she quickly sucker punched Blaque' on the side of the face two times.

"Chin check bitch!" Niagara smirked and held up her guard waiting for Blaque' to go wild... and she was right!

"Oh shit," yelled Blaque' as she was struck. "Now I got to kill you whore! Let me go, let me go Rique!"

"Go ahead... let her ass go! I'm not scared of that bitch. I got something for her! I'll beat your ass in your own shit; you can come see me anytime!"

Rique didn't release Blaque' because he was scared she would kill Niagara for embarrassing her. However, Niagara wasn't scared at all. She continued to yell insults at Blaque' and everyone, as the bouncers dragged her out of the club.

"I'm your doctor now bitch! That's right, I'm the bitch doctor and all ya'll hoes can get an appointment anytime! I got ass whippin perceptions with your name on it bitch! You and anybody that think... "

Blaque' didn't want to talk anymore; she struggled and fought Rique until he carried her backstage. The bouncers dragged Niagara out of the building until her voice faded in the background. Rique slung his sister into a small room, where she swung and scratched him once she was released. She paced back and forth like a hungry lion and told him to get out of her way. Rique didn't listen and stood in front of the door until she calmed down.

More people were leaving because of the ruckus, but regulars stayed because they found it entertaining. The night was wild, and everyone felt the energy. Donnie Cocherin grabbed the microphone and used the fight to his advantage.

"Now where else can you get mud wrestling without the motherfuckin' mud? This has got to be the Swingin' Cable Club baby!"

The crowd laughed and clapped at Donnie's poor attempt at humor. The lights dimmed, and the sound of a siren came over the speakers. Donnie looked confused because that was Officer Friendly's intro, but he continued. Donnie stood on top of a giant speaker as the red, white, and blue lights moved all around the club and made the introduction.

"Ladies... and some gentlemen; put your hands together for the dick that has sailed a thousand clits! Give it up for my main mans and them, Ram-Rock!"

Even after using Officer Friendly's music, Ram-Rock had the nerve to enter the stage in a cop uniform. The crowd went wild as Ram-Rock grabbed a cordless microphone and made an official announcement that he was now going to be called Ram-Cop!

"There's some swagger jackin going on up in this mutherfucker tonight," Donnie shouted jokingly over the microphone.

Since so many ladies at the club loved the cop theme, Blaque' had Ram-Rock change his theme to Ram-Cop. She wasn't going to lose a good theme like that just because one dancer didn't want to cooperate. Except for a few loyal Officer Friendly fans, the conversion was going over well that night, as planned.

"What the hell? I thought you got rid of Officer Friendly," Rique inquired.

"I did, however I still kept his music and everything else. When I said he left here naked, I meant it both literally and figuratively," responded Blaque', as she looked directly in her brother's eyes.

"Now that's cold. No, let me call it what it is... that's fucked up!"

"Why? Anyone can be replaced if they don't act right... that's business little brother." Blaque' smiled at Rique in a very sneaky and conniving way as she continued, "Are you gonna let me out of here now? I've calmed down. I'll kick that bitch teeth in at a later date. We need to get back to work and get that money."

Rique let Blaque' pass, but he stayed in the room a while to sort things out in his head. He knew that Blaque' was sending a clear message to him and all of the dancers that she would easily replace them if she didn't get her way. It was clear that even though the company started with Rique as the key figure, she had taken over. It was Blaque''s way or the highway. All of the drama wasn't worth it to Rique; he wanted peace in his life again.

As Blaque' stood backstage watching Ram-Cop's performance, she saw a man with his hat pulled down over his eyes approach. He jumped onto the stage, ripped open his shirt, and flung his hat into the crowd to reveal that he was Officer Friendly. Ram stood in one place looking puzzled as Friendly played to the women and took over the crowd. Blaque' motioned for Ram to do something from backstage, and an all out stripper battle began on stage.

Ram went to the same side of the stage and ripped his break away pants off in front of a woman that Friendly was playing to. Friendly in turn, slowly took off his jeans to reveal a g-string that read Dick 4 Dayz down the shaft. The woman and her girlfriends went wild, causing the crowd to side with Friendly. In an attempt to upstage Friendly, Ram-Cop picked the woman up and kicked her chair away. He buried his face between her legs, as he laid back on stage, until she was on top of him on all fours. The crowd went wild as he moved his head in a big circular motion like he was eating her pussy while underneath of her.

Officer Friendly was calm; he circled the woman, while signaling to the crowd that Ram was an amateur at eating pussy. He gave Ram two big thumbs down, then got behind the woman at the far end of the stage and flipped twice before landing face first in her ass. He shook his head wildly from side to side, as both the woman and the crowd screamed with excitement. Officer Friendly then quickly changed positions and simulated fucking her doggy style while Ram was still on the bottom. The women in the crowd began to throw money and yell I'm next.

"Man, get your fuckin' balls out of my face!" Ram got mad and threw the woman and Friendly to the side. Though he was embarrassed and wanted to fight, Blaque' motioned from backstage for him to remain calm.

Officer Friendly kindly helped the woman to her feet and grabbed a fist full of money off the floor. Everyone continued to go wild as he picked up the police shirt worn out by Ram, flung it over his shoulder, and strutted off the stage with his head held high.

Blaque' was angered by Ram's defeat on stage and said, "What a pussy; even I could have done better that that. I can see right now that I'm gonna have to merc me a nigga before the night is over."

Blaque' called the bouncers on her walkie-talkie to tell them to intercept Friendly in the parking lot and bring him to the back office. Once in the back office, four bouncers held Friendly until Blaque' came in. She walked in the room with a smirk on her face, and at the same time, a look of disgust.

"Look at you... you just don't know how to let anything go. You look stupid as hell standing here in a fucking G-string trying to play tough now. All I want to know is where is my cut of the money? You know the routine."

"Your cut? Shit, you better get your thong on and go to work then because this is mine; all of it!" Officer Friendly said angrily.

"Hold up, you didn't just dance in my club uninvited and say I'm not getting paid, did you? That's what this whole thing between me and you has been about; me getting a cut of everything! You don't get it. You don't fuckin' get it... do you?" Blaque' put her hand in her purse and walked over to him. She pressed the tip of what felt like a gun up under his balls and snarled in his face.

"Alright Blaque', how much you want?"

"You weren't invited, how much do you think I want? Please don't get it wrong because then I'm gonna think you're playing with me. I've already cut you enough slack for a lifetime. One more peep from you and I promise that the cops will never find your body."

Blaque' took all of Officer Friendly's money, made him strip bare, and had her bouncers throw him into the alley naked again.

Next, she turned her attention towards Ram-Cop. Blaque' sucked her teeth, shook her head, and said,

"Strip nigga! Take off all that shit, and you can get the fuck out too. Let this be a lesson that you need to take your craft more seriously. Don't comeback until you practice and become a professional!"

Blaque' had the bouncers throw Ram–Cop out right behind Officer Friendly. This finally confirmed that it was time for her to reign supreme in this game. Blaque' was ready to do some spring cleaning of dead weight, so that the money could grow and she could expand the businesses she created. The final piece of this puzzle however, wasn't going to be that simple because it involved her brother in one way or another.

Chapter VII:
Red Flags

"Rique, give me a call," there was a long pause in the voice mail message, "as a matter of fact, I want to say I'm sorry. I've never been jealous like that before baby. I don't know what came over me. Give me a call, it's Niagara."

The next morning Rique checked the voice mail messages on his cell phone; Niagara's was the first. It didn't succeed in making him feel any better about the commotion she caused. As a matter of fact, it made him more apprehensive. Rique listened to her ramble for a while then deleted the message and moved onto the next voice mail.

Diary Of A 12 Inch Brotha!

"Rique, this is Niagara again. I've called you about four times now. I know you've seen my number on your phone or at least got my message. When you get this give me a call. I need to talk to you."

Once again, Rique shook his head, deleted the message, and listened to the next voice mail.

"I don't know what or who was so important that you couldn't pick up the fuckin' phone after you got off of work. All I wanted to do was see you last night, and now I feel like you blame me for everything that went on. It's like you're abandoning me when I need you the most."

Rique hung up the phone after listening to Niagara's messages. He couldn't believe that she still thought he wanted to see her after all of the craziness from the night before. He didn't like her messages or tone and wondered what was up with her attitude. It was obvious that Niagara saw herself as the victim, but to him she was definitely the aggressor.

Rique left the club the previous night without saying anything else to Blaque', so he decided to skip the last two messages because he knew that they were from her. There was so much that was going on between them that he wanted to think before speaking to her again. Recently, on several occasions, Rique had been propositioned more vigorously than usual at the club. A lot of women and even a few men appeared to expect something more than a dance; one woman even asked who she needed to speak with for a little time with him. Rique always joked with his sister about her pimp-like

111

attitude with men, but it was hard for him to fathom that she would actually do it. It did inspire him to write in his journal though:

Entry # 105: The Pimp-stress

Dare I address?
The one and only woman I've ever met with talents like this,
Introducing my sis... the Pimp-stress.
Whether she knows it or not,
She makes money off of people getting undressed.
Yes...
It's only one step from sex, so tell me is that next?
Why take me from dee-jay to naked-ness,
But she said only in the third set...
The finale!
Now memberships at Bally's support my paycheck,
which to me is a trade for self-respect.
Naked-ness for a price,
I guess most men would love that every night...
but not me.
I would have never thought that a she,
would be able to pimp better than a he.
But a normal woman didn't do it...
It was my sis, the one and only Pimp-stress!

It was obvious to Rique that his life needed some major changes. The friction with his sister made him despise the business. The situation with the two women in his life was beginning to overwhelm his spirit as well. Rique wanted to have a normal day for once and go to a mall. He needed some time to think about the issues that he would eventually have to deal with. He had heard a lot of good things about Towson Town Center in Baltimore and decided that the unfamiliar surroundings were exactly what he needed.

Once at the mall, Rique walked around looking in the stores. Towson was a beautiful mall that exceeded his expectations and the atmosphere was friendly. While waiting in line at the food court, Rique noticed a man who appeared to be signing autographs in front of him. He wanted to know who the man was and waited for the right moment to strike up a conversation.

"You got a line, while you're standing in a line. You must be a bad dude homeboy," jokingly said Rique.

"Nah, I'm just chillin and taking it all in. I'm thankful that people even want my signature; I don't let it go to my head."

"So who are you? My fault man, I mean what do you do? I always get on my sister's case for speaking without thinking, and now I'm doing the same thing."

"It's cool brotha. I'm Dante Feenix, the author of the Black Butterfly Trilogy."

"Oh snap, the book about the mother who got framed for murder in Baltimore a few years ago? This honey I'm talking to just read part two. She couldn't put it down!"

Rique was familiar with his work because he too had read Black Butterfly, but didn't want to seem like a male groupie. He was really impressed at how easy going Mr. Feenix was because even local celebrities had big ego's these days, much less a national author.

"I'm glad she liked it, I'm finishing part three now. Here are two of my cards. Both of you can go to my website and cop it about a month early," Mr. Feenix replied.

"Thanks, I'll make sure we do that. So since you're an author and everything, does that make you a relationship expert? I got something I wanted to throw at you and get your opinion, man to man."

"Nah, I'm not a relationship expert but I'll give it a try if you wanna sit down?"

Both Rique and Mr. Feenix got their food then sat at a table in the food court. It was like they had been friends for years. Women kept coming by, flirting, and making conversation with Rique, something that an author like Mr. Feenix would notice.

"Damn Rique, you're catching eyes all over this joint It seems like the ladies are really feeling you out here."

"Nah, don't put that on me; it's both of us. Remember, I'm not the one out here signing autographs and shit."

"A'ight, you got me on that one, but what's up? Tell me your situation; I got a signing in like a half hour across the street."

"Ok, I'll give you the real short version. I got two honeys in my stable that are driving me crazy. The situations are totally different, but both have good and bad shit with them. Along with my job, my sister, and the overall pressures of life, it's too much. I need to cut one of them loose because I need to lighten my load. However, I want to make sure that I am fulfilled by the one I keep. So what do you think?"

"Let me make sure I understand what you are saying. You got two women you care about in two different situations, and you want to cut one back?"

"Yea, that's kinda what I'm saying. There's much more to it, but we on the same page," said Rique anxiously.

"Well Rique, the only thing I can tell you is that with any person there are issues. Sometimes good people are in bad situations, but make sure that you are being realistic about what you want. Is it something that a person can really give or is it something they choose not to give? In relationships we often try to make them what we want instead of seeing what they are."

"Wow! You sure sound like an expert to me. One more question, what if I kind of already made my decision, but shit is not solid where I want to be."

"Most of the times we have already decided where we want to be, and the other situation we use for spare parts. You get my drift? That's not really fair to the other person involved so shit never really works out. You need to analyze the person you want the relationship with and see why you needed spare parts to feel fulfilled to begin with. More than likely, you probably won't end up with either of those women though. Sorry, but I had to tell you that if you want me to keep it a hundred percent real."

"Thanks man, you are probably right. I need to get my shit together and see things for what they are but it's hard. I really don't have a grip on reality anymore, every since I started dancing at the club."

"Dancing at a club? Is that what you do for a living?" Mr. Feenix asked.

"Yea, I own an exotic dance troop and dee-jay business with my sister in DC, and I'm like the main attraction."

"Damn brother, no wonder you got the ladies. That's very interesting; I would love to write a story about something like that. My number is on the card I gave you so give me a call if you want to have a sit down because I would love to hear more."

"That sounds good; I was just joking about doing something like that. I even had a name for it... Diary of a Dee-Jaying Brotha," anxiously said Rique.

"Uh, that's pretty wack. Please leave the title to me my brother," Mr. Feenix laughed while Rique joined in.

They shook hands then Rique put his card in a safe place so that he wouldn't lose it. Rique could not believe that a national author was possibly interested in his life story. His mother always said that you never know what a casual conversation could lead to. That's why you should always network with people.

Rique's day seemed to be off to a better start so he decided to go see his mother and grandmother since he was already in Baltimore. Rique's mom lived on the eastside in a small single family home that was in a nice middle class suburb. She moved his grandmother in a few years ago when they sold the house that he grew up in. Rique knew he could always get a motivational word from his mother and spiritual guidance from his grandmother.

Rique walked into the front door of his mother's house, "Dang, ya'll don't lock doors around here or something? This must be Beverly Hills!"

"My baby is home! Ricky's here Mama!" Rique's mother shouted.

"Dang ma, you don't have to tell the whole world. I only stopped by for a minute to say hi. Hey do they still have that bible study at New Psalmist tonight?"

"Wow, I'm sure happy that you're asking that question. Is there anything wrong? You know mama had a dream about you the other day," said Rique's mother.

"No, there's nothing wrong. There doesn't have to be anything wrong for me to feel like I want to go to church. You raised me in church. Why do you think that there's something wrong?" Rique nervously asked.

"Look, I know my son and when something is troubling him. How are you and your sister's business doing? Why haven't either of you invited us to your office or even let me and Mama know what the business is? Why are you so secretive about everything Rique?"

"I'm not being secretive Ma. What kind of dream did Grandma have about me? Was it good or bad?"

Rique changed the subject and totally ignored his mother's questions about the business because he knew that she was hot on his trail. The more he spoke, the more she would get to the truth.

"I don't know boy. Why don't you go upstairs and ask her about the dream yourself? She's probably up there working her numbers out. Where's your sister? I haven't seen her in months. Tell her I said to get here, no more excuses."

Rique kissed his mother on the cheek to reassure her that he was alright, but it didn't work. She knew something was troubling him. However, Rique had to prepare himself for his grandmother because she was no joke. She appeared to have real psychic abilities at times and Blaque"'s strong personality to go with it. If there was ever a big mama that existed, she was definitely it.

Rique walked up the stairs and saw his grandmother sitting at a table in her room. She was writing in a black and white Meade notebook, as she cursed about random numbers.

"Hey Granny, how's my favorite girl?"

"Never mind all that, why haven't I seen you or your sister in months?"

"Well, I can only speak for me and say that I've been really busy."

"Busy doing what? That mystery business you and your sister keep hiding from everybody? Ya'll sure seem to be making a lot of money; I hope you're not doing anything illegal. I wasn't born yesterday ya know."

"No way Granny. We work hard, and that's all we do. I would never do anything illegal like sell drugs or anything like that."

"Okay if you say so, but I still haven't heard what it is that you and your sister do for a living. I know you wouldn't do anything illegal baby, but your sister sure would."

Rique's grandmother started laughing while she continued to write in her notebook. He never knew when to take her serious. One minute she was, and the next she was cracking a joke. However, no matter how much Granny joked around, everything she said was rooted in what she really believed.

"Stop playing around Granny. You know Blaque' would never do anything like sell drugs."

"No, I didn't say anything about selling drugs but she sure would pimp your narrow ass." Granny laughed again then continued, "Boy your sister would have you out there in a ruffled shirt and a tuxedo looking like Deuce Bigalow before you knew it! Pimpin is in her blood. When you were a baby, she used to charge everyone that wasn't in the family twenty-five cents just to pinch your cheeks. She gets it from me; I use to have dudes selling candy for me way back in elementary school."

Rique put his hand over his face and started laughing because he knew his grandmother wasn't joking. He watched Granny giggle for a moment, light a cigarette, and go right back to figuring out the numbers in her notebook. Rique hugged his grandmother, then kissed her on the cheek and went back down the stairs. His mother was in the living room cleaning the windows when he got to the bottom.

"No streaks please," said Rique.

"You better leave me alone before I get my belt," his mother responded.

"I'm getting ready to leave Ma. I got places to go, people to see."

"You know bible study is tonight at New Psalmist, your old church. Maybe it wouldn't be such a bad idea if you stopped by."

"Ha, ha, very funny but I told you that. Plus, I already told you Ma there's nothing wrong with me. I gotta deal with some situations and some people."

"Before you go, let me say one thing. If you want to know who your enemies are, move toward the good things and they will appear to hinder you."

Rique kissed his mother on the cheek and went to his car. While driving, he decided to take his mother's advice and go to the bible study. As Rique approached the church his cell phone started ringing, and he could see that it was Niagara. He was instantly reminded of his mother's words of wisdom by the call. Rique laughed to himself, changed the ringer to silent, and walked into the church.

After bible study, Rique felt renewed. It felt good to see some of the familiar faces at his old church. He began to think about what he needed to change in his life on his way home. As Rique pulled into his condo's parking lot, he could feel his cell phone vibrating. He knew it was Niagara again so he finally decided to answer.

"Hello?"

"Hey, I've been calling you over and over again. Is there something wrong? It feels like you're avoiding me," said Niagara.

"No, I'm not avoiding you. I just needed to do some thinking to clear my head and I did. I don't think that..."

Niagara cut him off, "I've been doing some thinking too and that's why I wanted to come over today, so we could talk."

"I don't think that would be a good idea because I'm extremely tired, and I really don't feel like discussing anything more tonight."

"There are some things I needed to say to you. I even have a letter so that I won't miss anything."

"Not tonight, I just want to be by myself. Please try to understand that Niagara."

"No, I don't understand why we can't have a mature face to face conversation and then I can go home. Why does everything have to be your way? You are a trip; you really are trippin right now," said Niagara angrily.

"I'm not trippin at all. I'm telling you the truth and that's it. You should respect that then maybe we could talk another day. I need a little space right now."

"Well, whatever! If you don't want to talk to me, that's cool. I'm gonna put this letter in the mail, then you can hit me up at your earliest convenience once you read it."

Rique heard the frustration in Niagara's voice; he could tell that she was holding her tongue. Rique decided at that moment, that he was definitely going to let her go because of how he was beginning to feel when he spoke to her. It was an early warning sign that was never wrong.

"That's cool; you can put the letter in the mail if you want to. I don't care."

"You don't care? That's exactly the problem. You don't care! Why can't I give it to you when I see you? It sounds like you don't plan on seeing me for a while."

"I don't know. I need to get my head together first, so I don't know when we would be able to see each other."

"Well, that's just great. I'll put this shit in the mail, and you can kiss my ass. There are some things you need to make time for. I don't understand why you keep pushing me away, but I guess it doesn't matter now."

Rique buried his face in his hand and shook his head in disbelief at how Niagara was speaking to him. He didn't respond to her commen,t so there was a deafening silence on the phone.

"Hello? Hello?" Niagara shouted into the phone.

"I'm here," Rique responded.

"Oh, I guess you ain't got nothing to say now all of a sudden?"

"What do you want me to say? Anything I say is going to be wrong, so I'm not gonna say anything."

"Fuck it then if you don't care enough about me to at least see me for a couple minutes so we can talk. Especially after you heard how upset I was! I feel like I'm begging you to do something you should want to do anyway, so like I said, fuck it then!"

Niagara hung the phone up in Rique's ear, and he felt instantly relieved. He wanted her to go anyway, but he didn't want to provoke her any further. To Rique, Niagara was like a confused little girl that blamed everyone else for her problems. She had been very needy every since he met her, which he liked in some ways but hated in others. He finally pulled into his condo's parking lot.

Chapter VIII:
The Doc 3

Blaque' went to her next appointment with Doctor Joyce. As usual, she wasted no time joking and laughing at the doctor as she prepared to lie on the couch. Blaque' pulled a wrinkled sheet of paper out of her pocket and handed it to the doctor.

"I had to steal that shit from out of one of his books."

"What are you talking about Blaque'? What did you hand to me?"

"You asked me to bring one of my brother's writings the next time I come, so there it is."

"This balled up thing is a poem?" asked Doctor Joyce.

"Yeah, I know. I just ripped it out when I got a chance."

"I want you to read it to me Blaque'; I think it will help you to understand your brother a little better if you spoke his words."

"Alright, but this is bullshit. I hate poetry. Here goes nothing; entry numba thirty two, it's called Untitled.

I write with such intensity; that it creates in me a need to be totally free... and heard. Every verb so abstract that at times, you can feel them tingle in every single nerve...

The symbolic gesture of the pressures of my verses... so non-rehearsed, they can quench a thirst without any curses. Feeling buzzed like a fifth drink, no time to think....quick sand as I sink, into this. You can feel the newness of every thought; because I'm on the verge of greatness... can you even picture this work of art?

Lateness to the horizon.... is a sin. So baby, where do I begin?

Trapped with you in a whirl wind, a romance of words, no apologies and no amends.... Check mate! Sexy you win... my body's affection, let's start. As I play the part of the fool for you... a romantic writer, the stakes get higher, so are you in boo? Because I've been inside of you... your mind, many times before; Act 1, Climax four.

Do you want some more? Say it then! Explore my potential. For in this writing, game, it's essential. As I endure your sweetness... growing pains, feeling softer. Remember, I'm your lover but first an author... of my life! I will record this. My credentials are on exhibit, so are you with it? A man can only hope because damn, I want it and I need it!

It's a bitter sweet taste; your sexy face and smile serve as my inspiration. Come on shorty; why don't you stay for awhile and experience true anticipation. You can spend the night, at my place of residence. Take one glance and it's pretty evident… that you're in for a treat. So place me inside of you… your mind silly girl. My life, my passion, will appear as a blur… fast! I'm so glad that we shared worlds but it won't last!"

"Wow, that was amazing Blaque'. What did you get from that? What does it tell you about your brother?" asked the doctor.

"I don't know? Sounds like sex. Sounds like a lot of things. Tell me what you got from it." Blaque' grew agitated because she didn't understand what the doctor wanted her to say.

"You're right, he is saying a lot of things in this piece, but for the most part he's making a correlation between sex and writing as if to say writing is as good as sex to him. The short time I spoke to your brother in the club, he wasn't the way I imagined. He was nice, considerate, and sweet like a person capable of writing something like this. Judging from his work, he seems to be a really sensitive person. Are you sure he even likes dancing or the club life you've drawn him in to?"

"Sure he likes it; he makes money and gets lots of attention. What man wouldn't want that?"

"Maybe your brother doesn't want that. Maybe his heart is in another place because it sure sounds like it to me. You really do need to have a sit down with him to discuss his interests and stop assuming you know them. People do grow up, and their interests do evolve."

"Okay Doc, I'll take it under advisement. Let's switch gears for a moment though. I want to ask you something about the other night." Blaque' began to giggle with a sneaky little look on her face.

"If it's not pertaining to our session, then I am not addressing it at all," Dr. Joyce said abruptly.

"Wait a minute, you are a real trip. First, you show up at my place of business uninvited… then get drunk, start a fight, and now you got the nerve to have an attitude with me? You have got to be kidding me!"

"I wasn't drunk, and I did not start a fight. That lame girl started with me for no reason. By the way, thanks again for helping me."

"You mean thanks for saving your ass, but don't mention it. I hate that bitch anyway, and the next time I see her, you can bet your bottom dollar they'll be pulling me off her ass."

"Well, make sure you get a few in for me because she was a real B, and I rarely use that word when it comes to my sisters, but she more than earned that title."

Blaque' laughed with Dr. Joyce, and the two women embraced. For the first time they were bonding, not as patient and doctor, but as girlfriends. Blaque' noticed that Doctor Joyce came to the club alone that night, even though it was her first time in a place like that.

"Why didn't you bring one of your home girls with you when you came to the club that night Doc? You shouldn't go to unfamiliar places alone. Didn't your mama teach you better than that?"

"Yea, but none of my friends would ever go to a strip club. They're all married or engaged to be married."

"How many friends are we talking about?"

"Well I only have two, possibly three people I would consider friends. The only reason I say possibly is because I just met one of them this year at my other friend's cocktail party."

"Cocktail party? Don't make me laugh. That bitch ain't your friend. She's your friend's friend. Whatever you do, don't make that mistake because if it ever came down to you and the one you met her through, it would be obvious! So tell me about your other two friends Doc."

"One is a council woman, and the other is a lawyer. That's all I'm sharing for today, so let's get back to you. Why are you trying to give me the third degree anyway?"

"I knew it; probably two plastic ass chicks hiding behind their degrees and careers that make you feel accepted as long as you appear to be on their level," Blaque' said decisively.

"You don't even know them. How can you make such a statement?"

"I know the type Doc. Would you mind if I called you Joyce?"

Blaque' moved close to Doctor Joyce. She looked around the office, shook her head and said, "None of this is you."

"Yes, Joyce is fine, but what do you mean when you say none of this is me?"

"I mean, this office is cold and not personable at all. I don't get that from you. You're a warm and giving person."

Blaque' moved even closer to Doctor Joyce. There was tension in the room because the two women had chemistry. She took Joyce's hand in hers and rubbed it gently.

Nervously Joyce responded, "I'm warm and giving huh? How do you know that? I can be a real bitch at times."

"Oh yes, I know you can be a bitch… but I like that too. However, for the most part, I see a sweet and conservative person with a wild edge that likes to explore. That's what I see. I could be wrong, but I doubt it."

Blaque' leaned into Doctor Joyce's personal space and ran her fingers along the nape of her neck.

"Blaque', what are you doing," whispered Doctor Joyce.

"Complimenting you. Is that alright? I have never met anyone as talented or as brilliant. You are the only reason I come to this office. I pay by the hour just to talk to you, so I can't even imagine why anyone like your friends or a man would squander the opportunity."

"You're going to make me blush," said Doctor Joyce as Blaque' continued leaning in and began to gently kiss her neck. "Blaque' wait," she said breathlessly.

"Wait for what? I appreciate you, and I want to show you how much I do."

Blaque' gently ran her tongue along the edge of Joyce's lips before kissing her and firmly squeezing her breasts, "I would have torn that motherfuckin' club up if somebody had hurt you in there."

"Stop," Joyce pushed Blaque''s shoulders back because she felt so overpowered. She fixed her clothes while Blaque' stood there staring and smiling. Doctor Joyce was extremely turned on but was uncomfortable with the scenario.

"Whoa, that definitely got outta hand. I'm going to have to ask you to leave Blaque'. I need time to process what just happened."

"Did I do something wrong Joyce? If I made you uncomfortable, I'm sorry."

"I'm okay. Oh, I don't know Blaque'. I wanted you to kiss me, but I have never been attracted to women before..."

"Before being attracted to me huh?" asked Blaque'.

"Yea, but I can't be all in my office making out with clients and shit. I need to be alone so I can collect myself right now. I want you to go, okay?"

"Alright, but I didn't mean to make you feel uncomfortable. I'm sorry if I did. Give me a call if we are still going to keep our future sessions."

As Blaque' exited the office, Joyce flopped down in her chair and buzzed her secretary to cancel all of her appointments for the day. She had a mixture of feelings ranging from ecstasy to disgust. If Blaque' and she were in a battle of wills, then she just lost by a mile. Joyce never figured the tension between them to be sexual, but now she could not stop thinking about sexing Blaque'.

The things Blaque' said about her were absolutely on point, and she seemed to have played on them to get where she wanted to go. Joyce had so many thoughts and emotions going through her mind that she didn't know what to do. Was she a Lesbian now? Was she going to go further with Blaque', or be openly attracted to other women? How was this going to affect how she dealt with other female clients?

She always kept her guard up against male clients for the same reason. Maybe she was over thinking the situation, and it was completely natural for a person to be curious about someone they admired.

Blaque' was attractive, intelligent, witty, ambitious, aggressive, and strong willed. She had many of the qualities Joyce would like in a man, so maybe it was the qualities she was drawn to and not the woman. Whatever the reason, Joyce had made her mind up that she was never going to see Blaque' again. She decided to grab her car keys and drive to Georgetown so that she could get her mind off of everything for a while.

Chapter IX:

What You Don't Know...

Later that night Blaque' received a call from Melanie. She sounded upset and wanted her to stop by. Blaque' loved Melanie and Dalvin's house because it sat back off of the main road deep in a wooded area behind a gate. She liked the privacy and always wanted to have something like that whenever she met her soul mate.

As Blaque' pulled up to the gate, it automatically opened and she could see that every light in the house was on. Melanie was waiting on the porch for Blaque' to get out of the car. She had her head down, and it looked like she had been crying.

"Hey girl, what's up? Are you okay?" Blaque' asked cautiously.

Melanie didn't respond. She just buried her head in Blaque"'s jacket and hugged her. Blaque' hugged her back and walked Melanie into the house as she tried to console her. Upon entering, Blaque' noticed that the house looked ram sacked; pictures knocked off the wall, broken glass, and things scattered everywhere.

"Mel, what's wrong? You gotta stay calm, don't upset the baby."

"Me and Dalvin just had a huge fight. I said some things, he said some things, I threw some shit then he ducked and before long it really got out of hand. I'm telling you, we were off the hook up in here."

Blaque' laughed and said, "Where is he now?"

"He jumped in his truck and took off like a bat outta hell. He was so mad Bee. I said some really mean shit."

"Girl you are pregnant. He'll be a'ight. What were ya'll fighting about anyway?"

"This..." Melanie grabbed the remote control from between the cushions of the couch and began to play a DVD. It was a home video of Dalvin playing around on a beach acting silly while he was getting ready to Jet Ski. Laughing hysterically on the video, Dalvin pulled the front of his trunks down and exposed his dick to the camera. There was no sound on the video so Blaque' couldn't hear anything.

"Yuck girl, I don't need to see all your man's business. Which vacation was this? Where were ya'll with the Jet Ski's, the beach, and all that shit?"

"I don't know because that's not me holding the camera. I found that DVD in my mailbox and confronted Dalvin with it."

"What the fuck did he have to say about it? His ass was cold busted right?"

"Well, we had a big fight, and he denied everything. He said that it was just him and his boys acting silly when they played the Heat in Miami."

"Oh that's bullshit! Then tell me why he's showing his dick to his boys. That's some ol' gay shit right there. You should have said that to him."

"I don't know; I can't see who's holding the camera and there's not even any sound on it, so he could be telling the truth."

"What girl? Um, I'm not going to say anything more because that's your husband, but who would put that kinda shit in your mailbox but some scorned chick? I hope you're right though because Dalvin is my boy, you're my best friend, and I don't wanna have to fuck him up!"

"Thanks Bee, I think. Girl, I said some pretty bad things to him that I should have kept to myself until I knew for sure. When I saw the video, I snapped because my emotions are through the roof right now. This pregnancy has got me all messed up emotionally. I think I'm chasing him away."

"Both of you needed to cool off. I'm sure Dalvin is somewhere right now feeling the same way and will be home soon to apologize. In the meantime though, you need to get some rest, and I'll clean up this mess."

Diary Of A 12 Inch Brotha!

Blaque' didn't give Melanie any choice because she grabbed her by the arm and walked her upstairs to the bedroom. As Blaque' straightened up the house, she heard Dalvin's keys jingling at the front door. He came in and went straight upstairs without even looking her way. After Blaque' finished cleaning up, she tip-toed upstairs and listened to hear any commotion. Everything was silent and seemed okay, so she yelled goodbye and left for the club.

Blaque' arrived at the club just as they were letting people in. The parking lot was full, and the line stretched to the main road. The popularity of the dancers always grew at a steady pace, but now it was like crack, through the roof! Blaque' believed it had a lot to do with her new sexscort venture. If word of mouth was the number one form of promotion, then she was ninety percent sure that the sexcorts would be something that women would spread like wildfire. The only negatives to the rapid growth were that she would need to house it separately and deal with her brother sooner.

Blaque' walked in through the back door and stayed out of sight. She wanted to see how everything would go without anyone knowing she was there. The dancers were playing around, security was lax, and the servers were just standing around talking. Tony was nowhere to be found, and no one looked prepared to receive the crowd that was outside. Blaque' clapped her hands to get everyone's attention before coming into view.

"Okay bitches! What the hell is going on here? Nobody's focused; no one looks like we have a packed parking lot outside! Why is that?"

"Ms. Blaque', when did you..." one bouncer said.

"Don't worry about it. Just get to your post and let's open the doors. Don't keep people waiting in the fucking parking lot. If you cost me money, you will get fired... so let's get busy everybody! "

Blaque' walked to the back where the dancers were to lay down some motivational law but noticed that Rique was not there.

"Has anyone seen my brother today? Is he here? What's going on?"

"Nah, he's not here and he ain't call either," replied Donnie Cochran.

"Damn Donnie, what am I going to do about him? I need you to host again. Go get one of his programmed CDs and load it up."

"Alright, but you know I might need someone to cover for me throughout the night... a-appointments ya know..."

"I know and I got you. Let John the Titan cover. Make sure the show flows evenly and smoothly. We want everyone to have a good time. This should not be just a night out at a strip club for the ladies; it should be a total erotic experience. That's how we get the big money. Never forget that!"

Blaque' went to her office so that she could call Rique and see why he was not at work. Once again, he did not answer his phone and Blaque' had to leave a message.

"Look Rique, I don't know what's going on with you, but the show is about to start, and you are not even here. I don't want to worry about you showing up every time we have a show. You could at least call and let me know if you're gonna be late or not coming in.

We need to have a talk about where we're going with this business because I can't keep going through this. Call me when you get this message."

Blaque' hung up the phone and went to prepare the club for the evening's show. She made sure the dancers knew their order, security was on post, and the door was ready to receive the crowd. Both she and the club owner, Tony, came to an arrangement that allowed Blaque' to get fifty percent of the bar in exchange for fifty percent of the sexcort take. Blaque' introduced the idea to Tony because she wanted to expand it and couldn't do that as long as she had to hide it from him or Rique.

Though it jeopardized his legitimate business, Tony went for the deal because he feared that Blaque' would take her whole operation somewhere else. He definitely didn't want her as competition because his club never made a real profit until she and Rique came. Tony decided to open a VIP champagne room for the women that wanted a private performance. Of course it served as a cover for the sexcort business, while Blaque' worked on buying the building behind the club.

As the night progressed, Rique didn't call or show up. Blaque' walked over to Tony and told him that she wanted to talk to him about Rique after the show was over. He said okay, but Blaque' could tell that it was a conversation he wasn't looking forward to. Tony liked Rique and didn't want to be caught in the middle of a family squabble.

Meanwhile, one of the bouncers had a special visitor at the front door, "Hey Greg, with your tight ass... you gonna let me and my girls in tonight?"

All of the bouncers at the front door, including Greg to whom she was speaking, turned to look in the direction of the voice. There stood a petite brown skinned woman with a plump little ass, a tight black dress, and a hot pink wig looking like Lil Kim in the nineties.

"You probably don't even remember me, but I remember you," she giggled. "It's me, Tina. You stopped me from going backstage to say hi to Thicke Rique the last time I was here."

Tina giggled some more with her two girlfriends, as Greg suddenly remembered who she was and began to laugh also. He enjoyed the attention, as the other bouncers watched him carry on a short conversation with the ladies.

"Yeah, I remember your little fine self. I also remember you getting into a fight that night."

"Yea, you would remember that wouldn't you. Don't worry; I don't fuck with that crazy bitch anymore. I promise that I'll be a good girl tonight Mr. Greg. You can spank me if I don't," Tina said in a baby voice.

"Maybe I liked the bad girl a little, not the fighting part of course, but your little sassiness is sexy."

"Well, I got a lot of sass, and if you drop the s I got a lot of that too." Tina swiped at her own ass to make it jiggle for him, and the audience of other bouncers watching them.

"Damn, I'd love to find out someday. Maybe I can get your number so we can go out sometime?"

"Maybe," said Tina as she and her girlfriends walked pass Greg into the club.

Chapter X:

Chocolate

The show began with the usual opening, except for one major exception, no Thicke Rique. The regular customers seemed very disappointed to Blaque, as she watched from backstage. She looked at Tony and shook her head, "We definitely need to talk before I address Rique because this shit needs to stop, and I mean now. These club rats are looking for him!"

"I know Blaque', but please remember that he's your brother first, and then he's the main attraction."

"You shoulda told him that because he's the one that always leaves me hangin."

Tony didn't respond. He continued looking forward at the crowd as if he didn't hear what she said. Donnie walked up to Blaque' from the dancer dressing room area and whispered that he needed to talk to her for a minute.

"The new guy Mr. Chocolate said that he wants to be down with the sexcort side of the business."

"I don't know about him, he seems a little reckless to me. He's always on testosterone overload, constantly walking around with his shirt off and shit. Does that boy even own a shirt?"

"Well, he is a stripper, so obviously he's comfortable being nude. Is that such a bad thing?"

"No, but it's all the time... even when we have our meetings. Plus, it's the attitude that goes with it. I don't feel we know him well enough yet. What do you think?"

"I think he'd be good, even though he has only been here for a short while. You're the one that said we needed another twelve inch nigga on the team just in case Rique is not down with the sexcort shit. So, I think it's perfect timing."

"Yeah, but we need somebody we can trust with our customers, and I'm not there with him yet. One damn ripple in the water and this whole thing comes tumbling down. Can he keep his mouth shut? Is he discreet? Does he know it's about pleasing the women and not himself? This is a business, and I need to feel I know these things about everybody that works for me."

"It's your call and you know that," Donnie responded.

"Alright, tell him he's cool, but wait until I say it's okay before you start setting him up with customers. Put him on ice for a while. I want to see how he act's around here just knowing he's a sexcort."

"I got you. I'll let him know before he goes on tonight. By the way, Rique called and left a message that he would not be in."

"He called you? Why didn't he call me or the club?"

"I don't know, he just left me a message and kept it short. He wanted me to tell you and didn't say why."

"Alright, that's some old coward shit there. I got his number, just like when we were kids, but this ain't no damn game. Go tell Chocolate he's on stage next."

Donnie went to the back room and got Mr. Chocolate. He told him that Blaque' said he could be down and that she would be in contact with him soon about it. As usual, he was hyped up and anxious to get started. Donnie saw what Blaque' meant when she said that Mr. Chocolate was on constant testosterone overload. Once he got on deck and prepared to perform, the MC began his introduction.

"Ladies, somebody told me that sweets will make you fat! So if you're watching your weight, maybe you should leave right now because coming to the stage is a brotha that's a pure su-gar rush! Get your sweet tooth ready for Miste-r Chocolate!"

Darkness engulfed the room, while soft red and white lights illuminated the stage. The smoke machine completed the look, as Darling Nikki by Prince played from the speakers surrounding the room. Mr. Chocolate walked on stage wearing a black Tarzan-like outfit with a bottle of Hershey's chocolate syrup in his hand. His dick dangled in a black g-string from beneath a fig leaf on the front of his costume.

Mr. Chocolate gyrated his way to the center of the stage, dragging a chair along the way. The women in the crowd were dancing seductively in their seats and watching his every move. Mr. Chocolate leaned back in the chair he brought on stage and began to squirt the chocolate onto his chest. The syrup slowly ran down to his belly button, as some women began to throw dollars onto the stage.

Tina walked up to the front of the stage and gyrated her little body with a fist full of ones, "That's my song, that's my song... do it baby!"

"Oh, it looks like you got yourself a fan Mr. Chocolate. Earn that money and show her how you get down," the MC exclaimed on the microphone.

Mr. Chocolate stared at Tina, as he stood up in front of her on the stage with the bottle of chocolate syrup. He popped the fig leaf off of his costume and was left with nothing on but his big black g-string. His dick was long as Rique's, but nowhere near as thick and wide. Tina put her hands in the air, swayed her hips, and began licking her lips at Mr. Chocolate. He paused, looked around the club, and held the syrup up to the crowd in an attempt to get them to yell.

All the women in the club, even the servers, focused their attention on Mr. Chocolate as he lifted his dick out of his g-string. He poured the chocolate syrup all over the head and shaft then began to stroke it in Tina's face.

The crowd roared with excitement, while Tina was throwing all her money at his feet.

"Yes, yes! That's what the fuck I'm talking about! Give it to me baby, oh!" Tina could barely control herself. She thought that it was extremely erotic and loved things like that because she wasn't getting it at home.

Tony, in the meantime, was yelling at the top of his lungs from backstage for Mr. Chocolate to put his dick back in the g-string! He did not have a license for a totally nude club, and something like that could bring unwanted attention to the sexcort business. Tony's rants were drowned out by the cheers of the women, so he made his way onto the stage and dragged Mr. Chocolate off with his dick in his hand.

"What the fuck are you doing?" Tony yelled at him once they got backstage, but it did no good because dragging him off made the crowd go even crazier.

"Listen to the crowd dog. Listen to them, they love me!" Mr. Chocolate walked off, pass Blaque' and back to the dancer's dressing room. She didn't say anything to him because she was still trying to decide if she was going to fuck him up or not.

"Donnie, Donnie!" she yelled.

"Yeah, whats up Blaque'?"

"I told you that motherfucker was reckless. You better talk to him before I do because it ain't gonna be pretty if he say some smart shit to me!"

"Okay, just please calm down and give me a minute with him. Is he in the back?"

Blaque' motioned yes and Donnie went to the dressing room to confront Mr. Chocolate. Once there, Donnie saw him putting on his clothes after taking a quick shower. Chocolate was fussing to himself about being pulled off the stage, while knocking back a big bottle of Hennessey.

"Yo Choc, I need to holla at you for a minute," said Donnie.

"A'ight, what's up, what you wanna talk about?" He said defiantly without even turning around.

"Man, you know we are not supposed to expose our genitals when we at the club. That's only okay for private parties and shit like that."

"Why is everybody making it such a big deal? I was feeling it, so I got a little crazy. What's the big deal?"

"The big deal is that Tony's license does not allow full nudity, and he doesn't want anybody exposing themselves."

Mr. Chocolate swallowed another big gulp of Hennessey then turned and looked at Donnie. He was partially dressed and took a bold stance which reminded Donnie of what Blaque' said earlier about testosterone overload.

"Well, I got caught up in the moment. I'm an artist, and that's what we do. I'm not like rest of these motherfuckers up in here, playing around and shit. I am a professional, erotic dancer that feels the music, so you can tell whoever to kiss my ass."

"Come on dog, you don't have to go that hard. We work for some real good people at a real good establishment. We got our own dressing room showers, food, drinks, and most of all creative control. They let us do just about anything we want within the rules."

"By people you mean Blaque' right? Cuz this ain't just about what Tony thinks. It's about how the queen wants it. Man, I don't know why ya'll walk around here like she's Al Capone or something. I saw her looking at me as I walked by. If she had something to say to me why she gotta send you all the time?"

"Man, cool out for a second. I'm here to help keep things running smoothly. I'm asking you, can you please tone it down a little so we can get this paper?"

"A'ight dog, I'll be cool for you, but I can't get with the rest of these motherfuckers around here. You know what I mean?"

"I got you, but it might help if you slow down on the drinking too. You were toasted before you even got on the stage, and I just watched you down that big bottle of Hen-dog."

"Woo, but that shit gets me right baby! I don't know bout all that but I'm cool. Right now, I'm bout to hit the floor and see if I can catch me a honey."

"Honey and Chocolate huh?"

"You know it!"

The two of them shook hands and left the dressing room. Donnie wasn't sure he got through to him, but at least he calmed the situation. A part of him felt that Blaque' was right about Mr. Chocolate, but another part felt that he was a good dude except for the drinking.

As the night progressed, Chocolate flirted and mingled with the women while the show was in progress. Blaque' blocked him out of her mind and vision because he really annoyed her. To her he was a chauvinistic asshole that needed to be taught a lesson. He was the classic type that could never see women in any other way but inferior... mentally, physically, and of course sexually. Being a dancer with women gawking at his body and giving him money for it only affirmed his views.

"Excuse me Mr. Chocolate, but I've got to tell you how sexy you are. I love your act, I mean your show."

"That's not an act baby. I really love the way chocolate feels on my body. That's the difference from me and these other dudes. I'm real, not acting at all when I'm on the stage."

"Well, I like it... a lot."

"What your name baby-girl?"

"Tina."

"Tina, that's cute just like you, simply adorable."

"Thank you, like I said... you sexy as hell too."

Tina stumbled into him, she had a lot to drink as usual and found it hard to keep her balance. Unlike Niagara, her new girlfriends didn't shun her drinking; they actually encouraged it because they were heavy drinkers as well. Though she was married, Tina liked to get her fantasies fulfilled with men far from home. She only considered fucking as cheating, so she never did that, but everything else was up for grabs.

"Damn baby, looks like you had a little too much to drink Ms. Tina. The real partiers are over here, tell the dee-jay! Me and my baby Tina love."

"I'm good; I just like to have a good time when I go out. What you got, Hennessey? You're a light weight; I only fucks with the Goose... straight. We had some drinks in the car before we even got in this mug."

"I heard that. Well, the dancers drink for free in here, so I'm about to get me some bottles and go to a private room to chill for a minute. Are you trying to come?"

"Well, I'm here with my friends and everything..."

"We're not leaving the building or nothing like that. We're just going in the back. VIP style, ya know. It won't take us long to polish off a bottle of Goose or anything else you want."

"Alright, they look like they're having fun anyway. Let's go."

Mr. Chocolate grabbed a bottle of Grey Goose and Hennessey, gave Tina a small bottle of Coke, and then they disappeared into the crowd without her so called girlfriends even noticing. He took her to a private sexcort room with nothing but a futon and two end tables in it. The room was dimly lit by a red light, while the music from the club played over the speakers. They sat down and began drinking as they felt each other up, made stupid jokes, and giggled like school kids.

Tina needed to use the bathroom, so he pointed her in the right direction and waited in the room for her. Chocolate had plans for Tina, so he poured her some

Grey Goose and dumped a powdery substance into her glass before stirring it up with some Coke to hide it. When Tina came back into the room, he met her with his drink and hers.

"Let's have a toast; to new friends and good times, Ms. Sexy and Mr. Chocolate."

"Well alright then, cheers!"

"Damn you are making my dick so fuckin' hard in this black dress. I'm about to bust something up in here."

"Oh, is this the part where I say let me help you with that?"

"No, this is the part where you say I got a sweet tooth for some chocolate."

"Oh, I heard that."

Mr. Chocolate unbuttoned his jeans and pulled his dick out. It was long, narrow, and crooked; more built for pain then pleasure. Tina remembered her episode with Rique to be more passionate than this, but she still went to work on it. She cupped his balls while taking long licks up and down the shaft like ice cream. At the top, she grabbed the head with her lips and sucked on just that area, while rolling her tongue around in her mouth. She then grabbed the shaft at the base and went up and down furiously with her mouth and hand.

"Woo shi-t shortie! Get that motherfucker right!"

Tina started feeling nauseous from all the drinking while she was sucking his dick. Mr. Chocolate, in the meantime, had pulled her dress up to her chest from behind, as she was kneeling and giving him head. He pushed his hand down the back of her panties and forced is finger in her ass… to her dismay.

"Oh! Wait a minute," said Tina as she scooted out of the way.

"I'm sorry baby, but I'm ready to give you this entire dick right now. Come over here and get on top of it."

"No, that's not a good idea. I'm married so I don't fuck."

Instantly Chocolate got mad, but didn't show it. He knew all was not lost because she was still drunk. He thought to himself, what a stupid bitch, she don't think suckin dick is cheatin. The mood was dying a sure death so he had to come up with something quick.

"That's cool baby, I can respect that, but can you at least finish the job this way… then I'll do you."

Tina said okay, even though she felt nauseous. She was so disoriented the room started to spin. She tried to make him cum quickly by sucking faster than usual when she resumed, but Chocolate grabbed the top of her head and started pumping his dick in her mouth until she regurgitated. Tina choked and gagged until she came out of her wig and fell off the futon onto the floor.

Chocolate liked what was going on; it actually turned him on and made his dick even harder. He helped Tina to her feet, but she couldn't stand by herself. The liquor finally caught up with her, so Chocolate opened up the futon and laid her down.

"Do you want me to get you anything? Are you okay baby?"

"No, I don't want anything. Let me lay here for a while; I'm so fucked up right now. Can you go check on my friends and tell them where I'm at?"

"Alright, get some rest. I'll be right back."

Chocolate pretended to be concerned, and only walked out front long enough to make sure no one was looking for her or him. Blaque' was mad at him for the stunt that he pulled earlier, so he knew that everyone would assume he was laying low for the rest of the night. Meanwhile, he saw Tina's two friends going to the pit for the grand finale, so he was in the clear for at least another forty five minutes.

Chocolate was sure to stay low key and calm, as he walked back to the room after grabbing his condoms and lube from the dressing room. When he opened the door, Tina was laying on the futon just out of it, with her dress hiked way up. He started kissing her belly and she began to move, incoherently mumbling words.

"Yeah baby, I'm gonna take care of you. I got what you want," he whispered as he pulled her panties off with little to no resistance. Tina's head was moving back and forth, as she kept mumbling, "Wait a minute..."

Chocolate took off his pants, kneeled on the futon, and put on the condom with the lube, "Wait for what baby, the Chocolate man is here." He snatched her legs up into his arms and dug his dick deep in her pussy while grabbing her wrist. Tina faintly struggled to no avail as he began to grind, vigorously which upgraded to a pound. Her shouts were drowned out by the loud music of the finale.

"Now let's play which hole feels best," said Chocolate.

Chapter IX:

What You Don't Know...

L

Chapter XI:

Reality Check

The morning sun peeked through the window of Rique's condo, while he lay on the bed and stared at the ceiling. He was thinking about his life and how different it was from what he would have liked it to be.

Rique had a successful business but wasn't proud of what it had become. He saw his sister almost every day, but wasn't close to her, and finally he found someone that he loved, but they were attached to someone else. Rique was spiritually perplexed to say the least; he decided that he was going to change his life starting today! The condo had been prepared to receive its lunchtime visitor for a little mid work day sexcapade.

Shyla was on her way to Rique's condo, so he planned to use the encounter as the perfect opportunity to clear some things up between them. The relationship had grown since they began two years ago, and it was to Rique's understanding, that she planned to leave her husband soon. Rique heard the door bell ring and someone playfully knocking rapidly on the door.

"Who is it?" Rique jokingly yelled as he walked to the door.

"It's your French maid service, here for your cleaning appointment."

Rique opened the door smiling; Shyla kissed him as she walked by into the condo. She started taking off her clothes immediately, leaving her shoes and stockings in the living room. Shyla was in a hurry because she was on an extended lunch break from her job as hotel manager at the Intercontinental Baltimore Harbor.

"Come on Rique, let's get it moving. I gotta be back in an hour. Why aren't you already naked?"

Since they didn't have much time, Rique decided to plant the seed of thought in her mind about leaving her husband while they were fucking. They could talk more about it later.

Rique quickly took off his clothes and followed Shyla into the bathroom. After she freshened up, Rique grabbed her waist from behind, while she still had one foot up on the toilet seat, and said, "Stay right there!"

He kneeled so that he could get up and under her legs to start eating her pussy while the water was still running. Shyla grabbed the sink, looked in the mirror, and started moaning as she dropped her ass down on his face repeatedly. Rique went from kneeling to sitting on the floor; he clutched one of her thighs and started matching her rhythm of up and down while he was licking. Shyla's leg started to tremble a little, so he stopped and carried her to the bedroom floor.

Rique liked fucking on the floor because it didn't give when he would hit the ass hard. He laid Shyla down and began to ask her questions about her husband, as he continued to eat her pussy.

"So when are you leaving him?" Rique asked.

"I'll leave him in two seconds if you lick it right there, in that spot again," Shyla panted. She thought Rique was playing around being nasty, but he was serious.

"Can he eat it like this baby?" Rique spread her pussy lips wide and began slurping and gently pulling her clit.

"Oh, oh, wait... shit!" Shyla jerked back.

Rique stopped then started again softly to prevent her from cumming, so that he could continue probing for information. He caressed her hips, while he licked in large circles all around her pussy and inner thigh area. Shyla moved her entire body, enjoying every minute of it.

"Baby, I want you to be all mine," said Rique as he extended one of her legs high in the air, so he could kiss and lick all around her asshole. He was really trying to turn her out and lean things in his favor this time.

"Rique baby, what are you talking about?"

"Let me know when we gonna do this for real. He can't eat this pussy like this; he can't fuck it like me. When are you going to leave him so we can get a place?"

"Okay, now you're blowin my high again. Stop it," Shyla said angrily.

Rique continued licking and holding her legs but then said, "You know that we belong together. I think the time is right for us to give it a chance baby. You said..."

"Rique stop, stop it!" Shyla turned and got up off the floor. "I don't know why you wanna do this now. You know I only got a few minutes here and you want to kill the mood with this."

"Baby I'm sorry, but here lately I've been thinking that ..."

"That what? That I need to leave my husband, my home, my life behind? That's not realistic and you know it," Shyla said defensively.

"Ya'll don't have any kids together, and we can get our own homes, cars, and everything else. If we're in love, we can have it all," Rique explained.

"Well, we don't have it all... we just don't. My husband is a dignified man; he's a respected attorney, and church board member."

"But you said he doesn't spend any time with you, he's always at church or working, and you didn't feel like a priority. You said I made you feel like a woman and that I was amazing."

"You are amazing, but we live in the real world and you're talking fantasy. Let's just say, I have feelings for you, but I still love my husband. You can't just walk away from a marriage." Shyla tried to convince Rique to see her points.

"You said you loved him but you weren't in love with him, and that we had so much in common. So why are you so scared to give us a chance? Is it because I'm nothing more than a stripper in your eyes?"

"No, but let's face it... you are a stripper. I never come to see your shows because I told you, I don't get down like that."

"Well, it sure looks like you get down like that at night when you call me. It's not a problem when ya'll have an argument, or when you didn't get that promotion last month at work. It wasn't a problem then!"

"Wow, I mean... wow. You really didn't have to put me out there like that. Like I'm some kind of hoe or something," Shyla said in disbelief.

"Well, what did you think you called me Shyla? I told you how I got into dancing, it was my sister. I only did the finale and never even went all the way nude. I don't have a problem walking away from any of it. I'd give it up for you in a heartbeat, but you're not willing to risk anything for me."

"Not willing to risk anything? What channel are you watching? I've risked something every day that I come over here! Put yourself in my position. If you had all that I have, there would be no way that you would risk what I have risked for you. So in my eyes, you're basically asking me to do something you wouldn't do for me!"

"It's stupid to have this argument again, when all it boils down to is what you're gonna do, because something needs to be done. I'm telling you right here, right now, that something needs to be done," said Rique adamantly.

Shyla felt like Rique was giving her an ultimatum, and she hated ultimatums. To her, Rique took for granted that a woman of her caliber was even willing to be with him in that way. He was aware of her caliber in the beginning, and even said that he never dated a woman like her before. Shyla was pissed off at his tone and his line of questioning. She paused for a minute to think before answering, and all it did was make her angrier.

"Ya know what? You win," Shyla spoke with contempt, "if you have to have it one way... you fucking win!"

Shyla grabbed her things, and kept repeating the statement, you win. She was extremely angry, and Rique had never seen that side of her before.

"What do you mean, I win? What did I win Shyla?"

"You've won the unadulterated truth! Since you want everything in black and white, here it is buddy! You, I care about, but your situation and everything that comes with your dysfunctional ass I don't want to be a part of! You said I was smart, educated, career oriented, independent, sexy, fine, and the list goes on."

"Yes, you are all those things. I meant what I said," Rique explained nervously.

"If you understood those things about me at that time, then why don't you understand that a woman like me would never want to seriously be with a stripper? The way you live your life is not for me. Your mentality about life is not shared, and the confusion that surrounds you would do nothing but drag me down! There it is... all laid out; you asked for it and you got it! Goodbye Rique."

Shyla walked out the door and left Rique sitting there with his thoughts. He felt like she had abandoned him, but deep down inside he knew she was right. Rique already hated those things about his life and sub-consciously wanted the relationship with Shyla to save him from it. Her decision was what a girl of her caliber would make, and Rique finally found out that no amount of fucking, sucking, kissing, or hugging was going get him what he wanted out of life. He was empty inside, and that has always been his real problem.

After sitting there for a while, Rique put on his jogging suit, track shoes, and went for a drive. He cried silently to himself, as he thought about his entire life and what it had become so far. He felt a range of emotions; abandonment, fear, anger, self pity, and pain. Whenever he felt like this, he would lock the world out and shut down. Rique didn't want to see or talk to anyone. He just wanted to sit in his room and meditate like a Buddhist when he returned to his condo.

Rique's cell phone kept ringing while he was driving; he never paid attention to the time and the fact that he was supposed to perform at the club again that night. He had missed many shows and really didn't care if he ever worked there again. The pressure and pain of his life weighed so heavy on his heart and spirit that everything else seemed small and unimportant. Rique remembered that one of his favorite places in the world usually had open mic night that day, so he decided to drive by and see what was up. On his way there, he decided to finally deal with one situation that he knew for sure was out of hand... Niagara. Rique picked up his cell phone, took a deep breath and made the call.

Chapter XII:

Hot Chocolate

Blaque' had been calling Rique night and day but could not get him, which infuriated her. She was planned on going to his house as soon as she got a handle on the Mr. Chocolate situation. Both she and Donnie were sitting in the car, as she talked to Tony on the phone, while waiting to meet up with her cousins.

"I agree with you Tony, we should not open the club until we feel comfortable that this situation is under control. We don't know what the girl is gonna do, but for right now she doesn't want the police involved because she's married."

"That's for right now, but what about her friends? You see how they were acting when they couldn't find her?"

"I don't care how they acted. They ain't shit anyway because they left her! When they couldn't find her, they assumed that she rolled out with some guy, so that's what she told them before she got home. She didn't even say it was Chocolate. "

"How do you know that?"

"Because after Greg found her in the room, he called me and we got her together. She wouldn't talk at first, but when I took her to the side by myself for a while, she opened right up. She started crying and telling me her life story. Man, I felt bad for her. I'm really gonna fuck him up Tony."

"Who?"

"What the fuck you mean who? Who do you think?"

"Chocolate?"

"Yea, it's gonna be hot chocolate once my team put some hot ones in that ass. You stay out of it. The less you know, the better. I don't think the girl is gonna talk as long as I stay in touch with her, but that motherfucker has got to pay! He gots to pay baby! Ain't that right Donnie-Don?"

Donnie nodded a very self assured yes, but was nervous because he referred Chocolate to Blaque' as a dancer in the first place. He feared that what she had planned for Chocolate might also be planned for him if he didn't go along with it. That was Blaque''s greatest source of power. People feared her because they couldn't figure her out. She was too unpredictable, and her cousins were some pretty unstable and menacing dudes.

"What the fuck? I gotta call you back Tony because my car keeps shaking up, and down and that can be only one thing."

Marcus was shaking the car with Blaque''s other two cousins, June-Bug and Stink. They all laughed at her reaction and got into the car.

"You were scared! June-Bug, did you see her face? You thought it was the Feds!" Stink kept laughing as they slapped five over the seat with each other.

"You know what... ya'll play too much. It hasn't even been five minutes and ya'll already bull-shittin. Let's get serious for a minute, okay?"

"My fault Bee," said Marcus, "Yo, ya'll niggas cool out and listen to Bee."

"A'ight, ya'll already know Donnie right? He's gonna help ya'll find this fool name Sean. They call him Chocolate; he used to dance for me at the club."

"So what this nigga do?" asked June-Bug.

"Shut-up man, damn! She gonna tell us if you let her finish. Go head Bee," responded Marcus.

"Thank you. This dude jeopardized my business, if you gotta know June-Bug. Is that good enough?"

"Yeah, but it really don't matter though. If you say he needs to disappear, he gonna disappear, and you know that!" Marcus answered affirmatively for everybody.

"Good. Well, this motherfucker needs to disappear! He could rat my whole operation out. I want ya'll to giv'em a case closer; robbery, gang related, or drug related. You know how it goes, nice and clean. Don't get crazy on me Marcus; we all know how you are. I need this to be clean, not a blood bath with tons of clues and possibilities for the police."

"Yeah, basically make it black-related... case closed," Stink interjected.

"Don't start with all that shit man," June-Bug responded.

"We got you Bee, so when you want us to get on it?" asked Marcus.

"Right now. Donnie will take you around. Call me and let me know what's up."

"Alright."

All the guys got into Marcus's car and headed to Chocolate's house with Donnie at the wheel. Marcus pulled out guns and ammunition like they were going to war. They appeared to be more organized than Donnie expected, like they had done this many times before. All three of them had black snow masks that covered half their faces, along with black sweater hats. Marcus seemed to get a rush from this and looked more anxious than his cousins to find Chocolate.

"So where are we going right now Donnie? Tell me what's up with this dude."

"I don't know much about him, other than he is from the west side of Baltimore and did a little time for some domestic shit. His crib is right around this corner, so I'm going to pull down the street a little," Donnie responded.

As they pulled down the street, Donnie pointed out Chocolate's house. Marcus made sure his cousins were locked and loaded with masks in hand. Donnie grew increasingly fearful about his own safety as he watched them prepare to bring about Chocolate's demise. The lights were on in the house, and there was a silver Lexus parked in the driveway.

"That's his ride. He's definitely in there," remarked Donnie.

"Good, I want everybody to chill for minute. Let's watch and get his schedule so that we can pick the perfect time to snatch him up. We might be here for the rest of the night if need be fellas, so tuck in your skirts. I need to know if anyone else is in there with him, so let's take a closer look. I'll get out while you guys circle around and pick me up on the other side," said Marcus.

Soon as they let Marcus out of the car, his phone started ringing. He cut it off and jogged behind Chocolate's house. The other guys circled the block as instructed but didn't see Marcus on the other side. Before they could slowly make their way back down the street, a police car came out of nowhere and flew pass them. It made a screeching stop in front of Chocolate's house.

Two men came running out of the house to the Lexus parked in the driveway. They attempted to get in the car until the police pulled their guns and made them get on the ground.

"Don't move! Stay on the ground! Sean Chocklin, you're under arrest!" shouted the police.

"Oh shit! The police are snatchin somebody up," yelled June-Bug.

"It's two of them. That's Chocolate right there but I don't think the other one is Marcus," replied Donnie.

At that moment someone banged on the car window, and everyone in the car jumped! It was Marcus with his hat pulled down way over his head. They opened the door to let him in.

"Damn, let's get the fuck outta here!" demanded Marcus.

"What happened? We was lookin' for you on the other side," said Stink.

"Yo Donnie, let's go! I'll tell ya'll in a minute; right now we got all kinds of guns and shit in here. Peel nigga, peel the fuck out!"

As they took off, Marcus cut his cell phone back on and saw that he had several new messages from Blaque' that said call me! Marcus even had a voicemail from Blaque' on his phone. He didn't listen to it or call her right away because he wanted to let everyone in the car know what happened.

"Yo Marcus, you must have some new voice messages on your phone because the top light keeps flashing. I got that exact same phone," Donnie remarked.

"Oh yeah I know. Dog, when I got out the car, I went straight to the back of the house to try and get a look into the window. Soon as I got there, I could hear his house phone ringing. By the time I looked in the window, he had dropped the phone and I saw two dudes running out the house."

"That's it?" Stink asked because they still didn't know anymore than they did before.

"Yep, that's it. We all know what it means though. He got a tip that the police was coming and he bounced. I don't know why the police was there, so that's why I'm going to call Bee to see if she knows anything new. June-Bug, please direct Donnie to our next destination."

"Our next destination?" asked Donnie, "I didn't think that we had anything more to do?"

Marcus didn't respond. Instead, he picked up his phone and called Blaque' without listening to her message. He had a bad feeling in the pit of his stomach about everything he had just seen, but he needed to talk to her about the second part of the plan.

Donnie followed June-Bug's directions, even though he also had a bad feeling in the pit of his stomach. Blaque' answered the phone, while Donnie tried to listen carefully to Marcus's end of the conversation.

"Yo Bee, shit is crazy on this end."

"Where are you? Did you listen to the message?"

"No, I called you straight back. We in the car right now, driving to the spot with Donnie. I gotta tell you what happened...."

"Don't say anything. Meet me at Columbia Lake... now!"

Blaque' hung the phone up in Marcus's ear. He already knew she hated talking about any business over the phone, so he didn't take it personal. Marcus had

Donnie turn the car around and take them to Columbia Lake, while everyone waited to hear an update of what was going on.

Once they arrived at the Lake, Blaque' wasn't far behind. She pulled up beside their car in the lower level of Copeland's parking lot and motioned for Marcus to get in her car. Blaque' looked troubled, and that made Marcus a little nervous because he absolutely had no clue about what was going on.

"Blaque', what's going on? The police came to the guy's house before we could do anything..."

"I know... the girl told her husband, and they went to the police. She named Chocolate so they went back and questioned Tony again. That's how they got Choc's real name and address."

"Dayum! So what do you want to do now?"

"I wasn't all that worried about the police finding out about what happened as I was about them finding out about the sexcorts shit. That's the thing that would bury me. Evidently the police don't know yet because they never mentioned anything to Tony, but it's only a matter of time until they do as long as Choc is still living."

"Oh, I got it... you think he will snitch as a way to get him off of the rape charge."

"Yep, it makes sense. It can't be rape if her intentions were to pay for sex, and we both know that she had no intention to pay that dumb ass."

"You gotta take him out before he talks Bee. I mean, that's the only way to protect your business and yourself."

"I know. Plus, if the police do find out about everything, both Tony and Donnie would have to be taken out. They could link all the pieces making it look like a big conspiracy."

"That's another thing; you said that we might have to take Donnie out. Do you still want us to put him to sleep?"

"I don't know if it's necessary yet. It could cause more attention at this point, but on the other hand it does close a loose end. How did Donnie act when he thought that you were going to kill Choc?"

"He looked nervous, but I would expect that from somebody that's never been in on a hit before. He didn't act that unusual."

"Alright, let me think about it. I'd rather be safe than sorry at this point, but don't do anything until I text you my decision."

"Alright, so are we gonna get that fool Choc before he talks? Do you want me to see if we can bail him out?'

"Nah, I want him to stay in there. This could be the break we needed; I can get him quicker and easier in there than on the street."

"How?"

"You know that money I give you every month to put in those four guys commissary?"

"Yeah."

"They aren't just friends. They're BGF."

"The Black Gorilla Family; are you a part of them?"

"No stupid, I used to mess with one of them, and he's pretty high ranked now. When he got locked up, I held him down and became a BGF sympathizer. They helped me fund my shit, and I in turn kick them doe monthly. You didn't know I was connected like that huh?"

"No I didn't know. So how are you gonna get word to them about Choc?"

"That's easy; they got cell phones and everything. I already sent the text and one of them should be calling me any minute now. I'll send the order out and that will be that. The only problem is, if they get to him in time."

"Alright, so what do you want us to do in the meantime?

"I want you to get with Donnie, and have him take you to see this list of dancers. These are the Sexcorts. See each one individually, not as a group, with Donnie. He will give them a message from me, and that will be that. Everything else, I want you to wait to hear from me."

"So what are you gonna do in the meantime?"

"I'm going to wait to hear the word on Choc's demise, deal with the po-po, and restructure everything. However, before I take another step, I'm going to deal with the Rique situation right now."

"I didn't know ya'll had a situation. What's up?"

"Nothing I can't handle. I think that this is too much for him to deal with. He's on some other shit. That's why I said restructure; it's time for him to just let this whole thing go. I can tell he's not in to it anymore, and he's wasting everybody's time including his own. He hasn't been coming to work regularly, so he doesn't even know about everything that's been going on. It's probably best that he don't know. That way I can just buy him out, and he can do whatever it is he wants."

"It's probably best; I never thought he was cut out for this. Hopefully, ya'll will still be close afterwards."

"I don't know because he really let me down. We started this together, and now it's like he disrespects me by doing what he wants and not honoring his obligations. There is no way we could expand like this. I really wish I knew what was going on in that head of his, but I'll soon find out."

"Well, good luck. I'm going to take Donnie to see the rest of your cake boys and wait on your call. Don't forget to give me the verdict on whether I should deal with Donnie or not."

"Alright, I'll holla at you."

Marcus got back into the passenger side of his car and briefed the guys only on what he felt they should know. He gave Donnie the list and told him what Blaque' instructed him to do. Noticing that his phone was dying, Marcus went to plug it into his cigarette lighter but saw that Donnie's phone was plugged in.

"Oops, my fault dog. I was trying to get some juice real quick," said Donnie.

"That's cool. You don't have to move it. This car has two cigarette outlets; I'll just plug mine in right here."

"Oh ,okay that's what up."

"Hey Marcus, can you or one of them drive so I can call these dudes before we meet with them?

"Alright, Stink will drive. Make sure you obey all the traffic rules because we can't afford to get pulled over Stink," Marcus instructed.

Donnie pulled the car over at a Seven-Eleven so they could switch seats. He went inside to grab a soda and a chili-cheese dog. Marcus sat on the hood of the car, while Stink sat behind the wheel, and June-Bug got out to stretch his legs. Marcus wanted to get some pussy after they wrapped everything up, so he asked Stink to hand him his phone so he could set it up. Without paying attention, Stink grabbed the first phone he saw and gave it to Marcus.

When Donnie came out of the store, Marcus was still talking on the phone. Everyone got back into the car so they could continue with their mission. Stink handed Donnie the other cell phone over the back seat so he could start make his calls.

They drove to meet each dancer personally. Donnie delivered Blaque"s verbal message of keep your mouth shut no matter what happens, and the presence of her cousins delivered the visual message of the consequences. The night grew later and later with each visit.

"Finally the last dude we have to meet. I'm ready to go home," said Donnie.

"Yeah I know, I got some pussy waiting for my arrival so hurry up," responded Marcus. He was lying back on the passenger side of the car with his hat over his eyes.

June-Bug blurted out "Man, I'm sleepy as shit!"

"Yeah, and I'm getting hungry. Can we stop somewhere?" added Stink.

As Donnie dialed the final dancer's number, a text came through on his phone. He stopped dialing and read, Don't put him to sleep yet, let him finish talking to the dancers. He's okay for right now. It looks like we are going to be able to get Choc before he talks. I'll let you know if something changes.

Donnie's eyes stretched wide as he immediately realized that he had Marcus's cell phone, and the message was from Blaque'. He kept his composure and went back to dialing the number of the final dancer. The best thing for him to do at that point was to remain calm.

Chapter XII:
Confrontations

"Baby you... are as sexy as you wanna be. But it really wouldn't matter if you weren't fine to anyone else, because you'd still be fine to me. Love... is a word that's so over used that no one really knows what it means. So unreal that you can only feel and see... makes you wanna sing off key, envy the birds and bees, call cupid stupid as you so desperately attempt to cop a plea... but there's no deal! For real, I've loved and lost and paid another's nigga's cost... because she was scorn. Worn... out, she tried to take another route, so sick of shoutin nigga get out, that she's breathless...

She didn't exhale or put her love up for sale, but she cheated... just so she could feel completed! She let me borrow her husband's seat and we drove until we were lost... now I 'm left to pay the cost because eventually she dropped me off... and now I feel empty. So tell me this, is pain the cousin of sexiness or just the Siamese twin of bliss? You know, attached at the hip. Man, what is this shit... that they call love?"

The crowd roared as Rique left the stage of Carolina Kitchen Bar and Grill's spoken word night. He had not performed his poetry since his college years so he decided to do it that night. Performing his poetry was like therapy to him because he could share his pain with an audience and it felt like they understood. The voice of one person can be judgmental, but the applause of many was comforting. After he finished his piece, Rique decided to go home and drink his blues away. As he pulled up to his complex, he noticed how silent and calm the evening felt. The night air was cool and blowing gently as if God himself was trying to comfort Rique.

"What the hell is going on with you," shouted Blaque' as she appeared from the shadows of his condo hallway. She decided that this would be the night to confront him about his disrespectful ways and the future of their partnership. In her opinion; Blaque' was fed up with Rique's continual missing of shows, ignoring of phone calls, and constant secrecy.

"Not now Bee... just- not- right- now." Rique didn't even look at her; he placed his forehead on the apartment door.

"Well when? When you wake up and realize that life ain't gonna wait for you? Or maybe when you see that these bitches out here don't love you, they just out for self? Or better yet, when you stop being so fuckin' selfish and realize that your actions affect more people than just you? Huh, will it be a good time then?"

Blaque' didn't care that her brother looked noticeably disturbed; she had a point to make and planned on making it.

Rique unlocked his apartment door and angrily threw it open as he entered his place of solitude. He had a lot on his mind and did not want to get into it with his sister at that point. Rique grabbed his basketball and sat down in his favorite chair. He began to squeeze the basketball in his hands like a huge tension ball as he shook his head back and forth.

"Yeah, go ahead and play with your little toys, like the spoiled ass brat you've always been since we were kids." Blaque' was a master at pressing people's hot buttons and wasn't going to stop until Rique said something to let her into his head. "Look at this place... candles, little statues, and all types of weird shit. It looks like a damn Buddhist temple or something."

"Leave me alone Blaque', I need to be alone right now..." Rique said in a low baritone while gritting his teeth.

"Okay, but please tell me all of this is not over a bitch, please. Tell me you are smarter than that. One chick is a groupie whore that don't mean you no good, and the other chick is using your ass cuz she's married and just want insignificant side dick!"

That was the one, the final straw that pushed Rique over the edge. Blaque' achieved her goal, "Shut up! Just shut the fuck up for one minute and be my big sister!"

Rique stood to his feet and threw the basketball to the floor, "I am not a male prostitute that you own. I'm not a cash register, a pimp, or an emotionless asshole sent here by the almighty just to profit you. I am your brother, your fuckin' flesh and blood!"

As Rique spoke his phone kept ringing. He could see that it was Niagara calling. He held the phone up to Blaque''s eyes and said, "You see this? You see this shit? I told her I was done with her, it was over, and to come pick up her shit today! Not because of you though... but because I don't want to do this anymore, any of it! That means the women, the easy money, the other dancers, the club and most of all... dealing with you! All I wanted to do was be happy for once. I finally find someone that does that for me and there's so much shit in the way, it's incredible. Why? You tell me why?"

"What are you tryin' to say to me?" Blaque' stepped to Rique and continued, "You quittin on me? Soon as shit get a little rough, you out? You made these problems and now you can't handle it? It's nobody's fault but your own. this is some weak ass shit you spittin! You got a responsibility to me, and if you don't shake this shit and get back to work, real quick... your ass will be done. Better yet, we will be done, and I ain't giving you shit because you are acting like a pussy!"

"Wow, that's all you see?" Rique asked sadly. "The business and the money, that's it? I don't know where you been all this time, but it's cool. I don't want nothin from you; I'll make it just fine. I quit and will never dance or do none of this shit again. My happiness is more important. If you're saying that I'm not your brother anymore because of that, then fine. I need you to leave because Niagara is on her way over here to get her shit for her departure as well. I'm cleaning out my closet today!"

Blaque' smirked at Rique in disgust, "You are a coward. Straight like that, no two ways about it. I've always been more man than you anyway. A damn woman is more man than her own baby brother. You don't ever have to worry about me again."

As Blaque' exited Rique's apartment, she could hear her cell phone vibrating in her purse. She noticed that she had an unanswered voicemail message. Blaque' was angry with her brother and said a lot of hurtful things to him as she often did, however this time seemed different to her for some reason. She attempted to block it out of her mind by listening to her voicemail message.

"Hey Blaque', it's me Dalvin." His voice sounded shaky and Blaque' was immediately alarmed because even though they were cool with one another, Melanie's husband never called her before.

"I'm down at the Georgetown Hospital in DC with Melanie. She was in an accident earlier today, and she asked me to call you. The doctors are with her now, so I don't want you to worry. I can't use my phone in there, so here is the room number, 213. Tell them you are a family member."

Blaque' immediately headed toward Georgetown hospital in Washington, DC. Her mind began racing as she attempted to call Dalvin back repeatedly with no success.

"Oh my God! Oh my goodness, what's goin' on today? Why would somebody attack Melanie, as sweet as she is?" Blaque' spoke to herself aloud often when she had a lot on her mind... When she arrived at the hospital she hurried to the emergency room's front desk, "Excuse me, I'm looking for Melanie Melody. I'm a family member, and I gotta call that she was here!"

The nurse looked at her computer, "Okay miss but please try to remain calm. Melani-e Melod-y... yes, she came in today. Have a seat while I call back to the nurses' station."

"Blaque'!" Dalvin walked through a set of double doors as the nurse was calling back. He was hesitant to hug Blaque' when he approached her, so he stood to the side and directed her back through the double doors.

"Oh my God Dalvin, what happened? Is she okay? Is the baby okay?" Blaque' couldn't stand to be in the dark on anything, especially something like this.

"She's doing well and the baby is okay. She's in that room, right there... 213. She asked for you." Dalvin didn't feel like talking. He just wanted to sit and collect his thoughts and emotions.

As Blaque' approached the door of the room, she realized that she's seen this image many times. Increasingly nervous about what she would find on the other side of the door, Blaque' clutched the cross around her neck and kissed it as she entered the room.

"Room service..." Blaque' whispered as she pushed the door open, "Anybody order a pizza?"

As the door opened, Blaque''s eyes began to tear because she could hardly recognize the woman lying in the hospital bed as her friend. Melanie's face was badly swollen, her right hand was wrapped almost up to her elbow, and her hair had been pulled back to expose a badly bruised cheek, two black eyes, and a cut lip. Blaque' shook her head no with disbelief as she approached the bed.

"Melanie?" her voice trembled. Blaque' couldn't stop the tears from rolling down her cheeks, though she tried by wiping them vigorously.

"Aw, don't do that Bee. I'm oka-y." Melanie's voice was slurred from her injuries. Blaque' kneeled next to the hospital bed and buried her face in Melanie's lap as she continued to cry.

"You're not fine. Look at your face, its... its..."

"All messed up? Come on Bee, stop it. The doctor said that the baby and I are fine. Plus, I thought you liked cabbage patch dolls." Melanie attempted to make a joke to lighten the mood as Blaque' often did but it fell on deaf ears.

"Stop playing Mel. Tell me about the accident." Blaque' insisted.

"Accident? Well, I don't really know where to begin, but check this out. I had just dropped Dalvin off at his little players meeting or whatever, and a car blew by me as I pulled out of the parking lot. I slammed on my brakes and was like dang, I can't believe that I almost got into another accident!"

"So they didn't hit you?" Blaque' asked.

"Wait a minute, I pulled onto the main street and saw that the other car had been stopped at the light ahead of me. While I was waiting for the light to change, the car in front kept revving the engine like they were about to take off. But when the light changed they didn't move, so the car behind me beeped at me and I in turn beeped at them. That's when it happened! The car in front took off backwards, directly into the front of my car. Bam!"

"So they were trying to hit you?" Blaque' was puzzled.

"I didn't know at that point, I was just so shocked. My air bags came out, glass was everywhere, and the force knocked my car back into an older man's car behind me. He got out of his car and ran up to see if I was okay. I was a little shaken up but nothing could have prepared me for what was next. The other driver that started the whole thing..."

"A little shaken up? Waiting at the light and backed into you? I don't understand... your face? Was he driving a really big truck or something?" Blaque' was confused because it appeared that Melanie had sustained far worst injuries than what could have come from the accident she was describing.

"No not he... she. She was driving a regular car; I think it was a rental car at that. It had a few stickers on it because when she blew by me I remember thinking that. I told the police it looked like a Chevy Lumina or Cavalier; it was definitely a midsized vehicle though. Anyway, when she got out of the car she began yelling at me as she walked up to my car, like it wasn't her fault! Bitch this, bitch that..."

"What? I wish I was there, I woulda..." Blaque' was so emotional that she kept interrupting but didn't realize it.

"Bee, please let me finish. When she got to the front of my car the old man from the other car cut her off and told her that she had some nerve to be yelling at me. Then outta nowhere, she hit him with the club thing you put on your steering wheel! Blood was everywhere when he fell on my hood; she hit him about two or three more times until he slid off the car to the ground. I took my seat belt off and kicked the car door out at her when she reached in through the broken window. Then I started the car but she made it back to the window and grabbed my shirt..." Melanie began to cry.

"Oh my God Melanie, it's okay. You don't have to re-live this, we can talk later." Blaque' tried to console her.

"No Bee, I'm okay. I can finish. While hanging out the window, she grabbed me by the shirt and all I could think of was my baby. I fought her off the best I could, but she kept punching me over and over again while she yelled, You think you special Bitch? You think you so special!" Both Melanie and Blaque' began to cry.

Melanie continued while Blaque' sat on the bed and held her, "I could feel sharp pains in my stomach so I threw the car into drive and sped off with her hanging out the window until she let go. I felt like she hated me and was trying to kill me but why? Cuz we were in a car accident? That doesn't make any sense to me, it's like I'm paranoid now." Melanie completely broke down and cried.

"Aw Melanie, I don't know why people do the things they do, but she's lucky it was you though because I would have ran her fuckin' ass straight into a wall! I mean it too." Blaque' had so many feelings going through her at that time, but the dominant one was rage.

Just at that moment, Dalvin came into the room. "You're up? Bee, can you excuse us for a moment? I need to talk to my wife."

"Sure Dalvin." Blaque' answered.

"Are the cops here? Did they find out any information on the car? Oh Bee, I forgot to tell you that in all the commotion I did manage to remember her tag number." Melanie tried to collect herself for Dalvin because he looked so worried about her.

"That's good Mel, I'll be on the other side of the door until ya'll finish. Let me know if you need anything." Blaque' didn't want to leave Melanie alone; she's always been very protective of her. To Blaque' things just didn't add up, and Dalvin was giving off some pretty strange vibes.

"Melanie baby." Dalvin's eyes began to water as he sat beside her bed and took her hand in his.

"Dalvin, you're scaring me. What's wrong? Did you get some bad news from the doctor or police or something?"

"No, I gotta tell you something. About a year ago, I was seeing this girl on and off in Virginia."

"When you say seeing her, what do you mean exactly?" Melanie's lip began to quiver.

Dalvin put his head down and said, "Yes Mel, it's what you're thinking and worse. Somehow, she thought we were in a relationship even though she knew I was married. I never..."

"You never what? You slept with her but you never what Dalvin?" Melanie interrupted Dalvin.

"I never meant to hurt you." Dalvin whispered as he shook his head from side to side.

Melanie's eyes started to cry, "So why are you telling me this now Dalvin? Do you think it could have been her?"

"I don't know for sure but I think so. Before I left her alone she had an abortion and claimed the baby was mine. I verified that she did have one but she didn't tell me until it was done, and she never asked me for any help, so I assumed she wasn't sure. I cut her loose months ago and she didn't take it well at all, as a matter of fact she got violent."

"Violent? Like what?" Melanie asked, with her eyes stretched wide.

"Everything was calm for a while until the sports caster congratulated me on being an expected father after the Orlando game a few months ago. Then I began to notice a lot of weird shit happening. My car was keyed, I felt like someone had been following me, and one night somebody cut me off like they were trying to run me off the road or something."

Melanie tried to be strong and sat up in the bed, "So what now? Why didn't you say something to the police when they were here? What do we do now?"

"W-e ain't gotta do shit!" Blaque' busted into the hospital room, "Just tell me the bitch name and where she at. I fuckin' knew it; you were acting too strange. I knew there was some more shit behind this!"

"Shhh Bee! You are loud, this is a hospital." Melanie tried to calm Blaque'.

As Blaque' stared Dalvin down waiting for an answer, a nurse walked in with a look of annoyance on her face.

"Excuse me Ms. Melody, but an officer Thomas is here to see you. Is now a good time?"

"Now would be perfect!" Blaque' answered for Melanie.

"Blaque', I asked you to stop. Yes, it's okay nurse. You can send him in, thank you."

As the nurse exited, Officer Thomas came in talking and looking down at his note pad, "Alright, we got the car and you were right…"

Officer Thomas looked up and immediately stopped talking when he saw all three people staring at him and hanging on his every word.

"It's okay Officer Thomas, keep going because we were just talking about this ourselves." Melanie assured the officer.

"Well, you were right when you said it was a rental. It was rented from Rent-a-Wreck two days ago by a Miss Pigford... Niagara Pigford."

Blaque' and Dalvin's face went blank; they both began to shake their heads in disbelief.

"Dalvin, is that her?" Melanie asked.

"Yeah, that's her. I can't believe this. I can't believe that she would go this far with all of this." Dalvin said shockingly.

"Wait, you know her Mr. Melody?" Officer Thomas asked.

"Yeah, I know her. I just didn't want to believe it, she is really crazy. She actually told me that it wouldn't be over until she said it's over and that she wouldn't be the only one hurting."

"I don't understand Mr. Melody," Officer Thomas waited for a response while Blaque' stood there with her hands over her mouth listening.

"I had a fling with her and then broke it off, but I didn't think that she was capable of this."

"Anyone is capable of violence Sir. That's the first thing you learn in my line of work. However, this girl has a violent history. On my way over here, I punched her name into the computer just to see if anything came up, and she currently has a warrant for a bar related stabbing among other things on her record."

"What!" Blaque' shouted in fear, anger, and surprise. She had so many emotions going through her at once that she was shaking.

"That can't be the same girl your brother is messin with Blaque'?" Melanie asked.

"How many Niagara's do you know Mel? Dalvin, was that girl light skin, kinda tall, with black hair and a big butt?"

"Yeah, what's this about your brotha?" Dalvin asked curiously.

Blaque' pulled out her cell phone and called Rique immediately. "Oh shit, that bitch left your Jersey over my brother's house. He just dumped her and told her to come get her shit from his house! I gotta warn him." Blaque' hurried out of the room pass everybody. Rique's phone rang a while then went straight to voice mail every time she called.

"Where does he live?" Officer Thomas yelled.

"Don't go by yourself Blaque'; wait for somebody to go with you!" Melanie shouted as Blaque' took off running out of the room.

Blaque' yelled the address back to them as she ran down the hospital hallway to the steps. Everyone was shouting wait, but she had already taken off at top speed, skipping the option of the elevator. Dalvin, Melanie, and Officer Thomas tried to piece together the address from what Blaque' shouted back to them, but could only agree on the street and what hundred block they heard.

Melanie's heart started beating fast as she became more stressed and scarred for her friend. Her heart monitor began to beep loudly before two nurses ran into the room and asked the gentlemen to leave.

"Mrs. Melody, please calm down. Remember the baby can feel what you feel. You have to calm down. Somebody go get the doctor, now!"

One nurse yelled to everyone as the other pushed Dalvin and Officer Thomas out of the room. The Officer called in the street address as best he could before leaving the hospital, while Dalvin waited in the lobby to see Melanie again. His heart was on fire because he never thought that the situation with Niagara would have ever one this far and hurt so many people.

Chapter IX:
What You Don't Know...

L

Chapter XIV:

Baby...

After Rique packed a few of Niagara's things into a
giant trash bag, he sat it near the front door of his condo.
Rique began to reflect on his life again and realized that a
major source of his pain was trying to please everyone
but himself.

"Damn, how the hell did I get here? How did I go
from DJ to stripper? How did I go from pursuing my
passion to being fucked up in the game?" Rique talked
aloud to himself as he cleaned his apartment and waited
for Niagara.

"So let me get this straight in my head, I spun
records at a local strip club just so I can make more
money to keep Dee-Jaying, but then... I end up being a

stripper. I took my sister on as a partner so that we could be closer but then… the business divided us. I finally met a woman that I thought was perfect for me but she's married and doesn't take me serious because… I'm a stripper." Rique's home phone began to ring. He picked up the cordless handset and stared at the caller-id. "What the hell does Blaque' want?

Rique put his hand over his face and shook his head as he heard the doorbell ring to his apartment. "And now, I'm about to hurt the feelings of someone that has been nothing but fun. That's it; today I've finally learned my lesson."

Rique opened the door and there stood Niagara with her head down wearing black sun glasses and a black jacket zipped to the top.

"Did you get around to reading the letter yet?"

"Naw, it's on the coffee table. You can say whatever you have to say to me now; I'm not for all these games you playin," Rique said doubtfully.

"Well then, can I come in for a minute please? We need to talk."

Rique moved out of her path so that she could enter. Niagara's voice sounded shaky as if she was nervous or had been crying. Rique stood in the center of the living room near the coffee table where he sat his keys, cell phone, and old mail. The tension in the room was thick, silence made every sound amplified a thousand times. Suddenly Rique's cell phone rang; he picked it up and could see that Blaque' was calling him again.

"Wait... before you answer that, can I please just have one final moment of uninterrupted time with you? Please let me say what I have to say and I'll be out of your hair, okay?"

Rique sat the phone back on the coffee table, stuck his hands in his pockets, and said, "I'm listening."

"What's wrong Rique? Tell me... what's wrong?" Niagara kept her head down and continued not to look at Rique.

"Niagara, my life is just not what I would like..."

"No, I mean with me..." her tone began to sound more desperate, "With me, with me, with...me!"

Niagara lifted her head and looked at Rique from behind her dark shades. She pushed her hands deep inside the pockets of her jacket, as she shook her head back and forth, with a snarl imprinted on her face.

Rique attempted to dismiss Niagara, thinking that this was just another case of a woman that couldn't handle rejection. "Look sweetie pie, there's nothing wrong with you, and there's nothing wrong with me. Our time has come and gone, that's it, so move on."

"I asked you a question," Niagara grinded her teeth together as she stepped slightly closer to Rique. "Don't fuckin' dismiss me!"

"So now you gonna start trippin and playing the victim right? That's okay, I'm not even gonna sweat it because this is exactly what I expected. Listen to me, I'm throwing my old way of life totally away... and that includes you. I'm sorry if you don't understand... but right now you need to start moving toward the door."

Rique's cell phone buzzed with a text message that gave him a much needed distraction. "I don't owe you or anybody an explanation! All this has drained me, and I'm just done… so get over it!" Rique saw that the text was from Blaque', so he took his eyes off of Niagara and began to read.

"Yo, The bitch Niagara is crazy!!!! If she comes to your house before I get there, DON'T LET HER IN!!!! I'll explain when I see you."

"Get over this, you motherfuckin' asshole!" Niagara lunged at Rique with a large knife she pulled from her jacket. She stabbed him two times deep in his shoulder blade before being knocked away.

Rique immediately grabbed his shoulder and fell to the floor. He kicked the coffee table between himself and Niagara. Rique could barely move his arm as the blood began to flow heavily. Niagara quickly walked to the front door and grabbed the metal baseball bat from behind it.

"A nigga knocka huh? You're supposed to use this for intruders right?" A thief in the night, that's what you are. All men, as a matter of fact, just two bit thieves in the night! How many nights motherfuckers like you tried to steal my body with their hands, my hopes with fake ass promises, and my mind with vicious lies? How many…huh? How many fuckin' nights have you stole!" Niagara yelled at Rique in rage at the top of her lungs.

Again, she lunged at Rique over the coffee table. Niagara began to swing the bat wildly with all her might, hitting him on the side of the face and arms when he attempted to block his wounded shoulder. The blunt trauma was coming from every direction so Rique yelled in agonizing pain with fear that she may actually kill him if no one intervened soon. Neighbors began to bang on the door in an attempt to break it down, but Rique's many locks and reinforcements proved to be even sturdier than hoped.

As Blaque' arrived, she double parked, grabbed her purse and ran quickly to Rique's apartment. She could hear people yelling and saw a crowd starting to form in front of Rique's door.

"Shit, I told him about that damn door. Ya'll can't get in?" Blaque' yelled to the men at the front of the crowd that was trying to break the door down.

"Naw, not yet. This shit is like Fort Knox man. Anybody got a crow bar?" The man asked.

Blaque' could hear things crashing inside the condo and lots of yelling, so she quickly darted to the rear of the building. The crowd at Rique's door was finally starting to see some light! Niagara could hear them crashing away at the door and could see that they were almost in. She grabbed the knife and carried the bat with her as she ran to the window where the fire escape was located.

"One... two... three!" The crowd of people yelled in unison before crashing into the door the final time. They all paused for a minute fearing what they would see. The debris from the door and the frame made a cloud of dust; however all they could see and smell was blood as Rique laid lifeless on the floor in a pool.

When Niagara made it down to the final seven steps on the fire escape, she saw Blaque' standing at the bottom in the alley. Niagara's hands and shirt were covered with blood, and it looked like she had been sweating profusely. Niagara raised the knife and bat toward Blaque' before saying, "I'm warning you... get out of my way."

"Now I know... that you are fuckin' crazy! Beyond a shadow of a doubt, sure as my name is Blaque', I am packin' the mutherfuckin' heat to the third degree!"

Blaque' let her purse drop to the ground to reveal her hand wrapped around the handle of a shiny black 9mm handgun.

They could hear the police and paramedic sirens approaching as the sound of people in Rique's condo spilled into the alley. Blaque' saw that her brother's blood smeared the bat and knife Niagara was holding.

Niagara looked down to the end of the alley for the police and said, "So that's it. Looks like I'm gonna have to drop it..."

"No, keep it!" whispered Blaque'.

Bang!

Blaque' shot Niagara in the shoulder. She watched her drop the weapons, spin around, and fall down to the last step of the fire escape. She stood over Niagara with the gun pointed at her head, and foot perfectly planted on her wound. Niagara screamed in pain as Blaque' applied pressure with tears rolling down her cheeks.

"I purposely didn't kill you because I wanted to suffer. If my brother is dead from what you did, I promise you that I will put every dollar I got on your brain in jail... and my word is definitely bond!"

"Freeze! Don't move! Drop your gun now!" The police yelled from a distance down the alley way.

Blaque' started shaking because she wasn't one hundred percent sure she wanted to let Niagara go yet. She didn't know how badly her brother was hurt or even if he was dead.

"I said no-w! Get down on the ground!" The officer yelled again as all of them took aim at Blaque'.

One of the residents looked out of their apartment window into the alley and yelled down to the cops.

"That's his sister! She's not the one, it's the other one. That is his sister!"

Blaque' lowered the gun, then sat it on the ground and kicked it toward the cops. She never looked away from Niagara as the cops slowly approached both of them.

Niagara was slowly trying to get up when Blaque' jumped on top of her and began to squeeze her neck with all of her might. "This is just so you know, just so you know bitch!"

The police grabbed Blaque' and pulled her off of Niagara as she crawled and gasped for a few breathes of air.

Chapter XV:

Revelations

A few months later… "I'm so nervous Bee. Why did he choose me? I'm really not ready; there are so many people that deserve this honor over me. Pastor T is trippin." Rique sat down and nervously rubbed his hands together while Blaque' attempted to straighten his tie.

"Well, ya look good. Why are you trippin? The reverend asked you to join him in the pulpit; obviously he sees something in you." Blaque' tried to calm Rique.

"I don't know Bee, something just seems different today." Rique paused and stared at Blaque' for a minute. "Thanks for coming to church with me today and bringing Melanie. I'm so glad she is gonna work things out with Dalvin because God is the only way it's gonna get right. Oh and one more thing, thanks for nursing this bag of bones back to health. I'll sure be glad when I get all of my weight back."

"Well, you lost a lot of blood, give yourself time. Besides, you the only bag of bones I got. Sike, I love you and it's just time for me to start acting like a big sister around here. It's a shame that it took something like what we went through for me to realize it." Blaque' hugged Rique.

"Yeah, I love you too. But it's not over yet; we still gotta go to court and see that crazy chick one last time. You for kickin butt and me for getting my butt kicked." Rique chuckled for a second then got serious. "Bee, something has been on my mind and I think that here is as good a place as any to talk about it."

"What's up? Make it quick though, the pastor said he wanted you on stage in a couple of minutes."

"Well, before I saw Niagara that day at my condo she had sent me a letter. I never got around to opening it before everything happened, so I did once I finally got out of the hospital. It was a long letter that started with how much she loved me but got angrier as it went on. Telling me that I didn't know a good thing when I saw one, this and that... you know goes with people. By the end though, she said that she was pregnant with my baby and I had better step-up and be a man or there would be hell to pay."

Rique stopped because Blaque' had a scary look on her face.

"Rique, when I told Tony that we were quitting the business, he gave me some mail that came to the club for me. One was unmarked and had a card in it that said Auntie! That's it; nothing else was on the card. We should turn that stuff over to the district attorney. Let me ask you though, do you think she was even pregnant?"

"That's what I wondered at first, but then I didn't give it much thought until my lawyer said something about a baby to me. She's definitely pregnant, but I don't think it's mine. Think about it, she was sleeping with a married NBA player and a stripper, how many other dudes could have been in the line up?"

"Yeah, you're right," said Blaque'.

"Bee, you know she's out on bail... right?"

"I can't believe they gave her bail, after all that shhh... oops! I mean stuff. It had to be some old high as hell number that they thought she couldn't post."

"Yeah I know... that blew my mind when I found out. You know the detective told me last week that they found six different blood types between her clothes and the knife. Mine, hers, Melanie's, the man at Melanie's car, and yours were all on her things. The case is a slam dunk so far but they can't figure out where the sixth blood type came from," Rique said nervously.

"Boy, you can't do anything about that right now. Let's go out here and praise God. He'll work it out, put it in his hands! He already saved your dumb self once, he can do it again." Blaque' laughed as she took Rique by the arm and guided him to the pulpit.

Diary Of A 12 Inch Brotha!

When Rique came out onto the stage, he could see tons of people crying and praying from the sermon. Rique nervously sat in a chair left for him on the right side of the stage, beside three other men. Deacon Daryl, the most radical of the pastor's board, approached Rique and the three men and said, "Okay brothers, when the pastor calls the men to the alter we want you to go and receive them. Approach the crowd from the stage, simply bow your head, stretch out your hands palms up, and say I am my brother's keeper, what would you like to leave at the altar tonight."

Rique's nerves were at a fever pitch; he looked out at the crowd and saw Blaque', Melanie, and even Dalvin sitting there in support of him. He reflected on his life and began to weep like many of the people he was supposed to receive. Rique wanted to leave, but remained as he waited for the pastor to finish the altar call.

"Since tonight's message here at LFCC, was being your brother's keeper, we are going to have a special altar call tonight. It's time for the men to stand up! So often it's the women getting saved, when it's the men that need it most. So tonight, I want each and every man that's ready for a change, to come up here and place his hands into one of the brothers' hands on the stage. Then tell him what you were struggling with, hurting from, or would like to leave here at the altar. Remember, when the world pushes you to your knees, you're in the perfect position to pray. God is going to perform a miracle here today. I can feel it!!!"

Rique stood up and moved to the front of the stage. There was a sea of men from all walks of life surrounding the stage in packs. Rique grew more and more nervous with each step as he approached the crowd at the edge of the stage. He put his head down, took a deep breath, and stuck his hands out. Immediately, a man lightly placed his hands into Rique's.

"I am my brother's keeper. What would you like to leave at the altar?" asked Rique reluctantly.

The man initially didn't say anything he just stood there with his head down crying. Rique could feel the tears from the man's eyes falling on to his wrist. He could feel the man's grip tighten and a tremendous spiritual energy take him over. Rique lifted his head and said to the man in a more honest tone, "I am my brother's keeper. Please, tell me what's wrong with you brother?"

Finally the man spoke, "I am struggling with the demon of unforgive-ness. I recently resigned as deacon from my church, took a forced leave of absence from my job, and even contemplated suicide. All because my wife confessed to me that she had been having an affair for almost two years."

Rique felt sorry for the man, so he pulled him up on stage and walked him to the private green room and said, "I know things seem bad brother but that's no reason to destroy or take your own life."

"Brother, please let me finish. The only reason she told me about the affair was because she found out that she was pregnant and didn't know who the baby belonged to. She said that she broke it off with him before she knew, but I was just way too angry so I moved out.

She begged me not to leave her because she was scared and thought that someone had been following her to the doctor appointments. I thought it was just a ploy to keep me until one day, a few months ago, my wife was found dead in our house from numerous knife wounds to the stomach!" The man let out a loud cry and fell to the floor screaming, "I'm so sorry I wasn't there baby! I miss you Shyla! God help me, please. Shyla-a-a-a!"

Pastor T and the deacons ran into the greeting room and grabbed the man while he lay on the floor crying his eyes out. Deacon Daryl grabbed Rique by the arms as he stood in the corner in shock.

"Rique, what happened? Why is this guy going crazy like that?" Deacon Daryl watched Rique slowly breakdown just as the man did. Tears began to roll down his cheeks as he ran out the emergency exit doors with his face covered.

When Rique got to his car he drove straight to Columbia Lake in Howard County. He didn't play any music because he wanted to sit in silence and remember Shyla. Rique grabbed his journal from the glove compartment of his car and began to read his own poems from beginning to end. They chronicled his many relationships because each poem was linked to a different woman. The journal made clear to him that his whole life had been about trying to find love through numerous sexual encounters. Rique could see how emotionally messed up he was by the time he got to the poems about Shyla.

Rique had never found love and his journal made that clear to him, he now had mixed emotions about the book. On one hand; he wanted to destroy it because it once served as a refuge, but it was now a reminder of his own confusion and self-torment. He hated it. On the other hand, it chronicled his life up to a moment of clarity that he thought men everywhere could benefit from, so it could possibly serve a purpose. Rique decided to let someone else make the decision for him, so he drove to the post office and made a call from the parking lot.

"Hello? Damn, it's his voicemail!" Rique was frustrated but decided to leave a message anyway.

"Hi this is Rique; I met you at the Towson Mall the other day. You told me to give you a call if I wanted to talk about my life possibly for a book. Well, I'm ready to share some real heavy situations with you if you have the time. The best place to start is with the poems in my journal because they kinda logged my story as it happened. I'm going to mail it to the address on the card you gave me right now. Please don't let anyone else read it because you're the only one I'm revealing it to. If you are interested holler back, if not, trash it because I really don't want the memories man, thank you Mr. Feenix."

THE END

Diary Of A 12 Inch Brotha!

"When life pushes you to your knees, you're in the perfect position to pray."

-DF/x

**Available Everywhere by
Dante' Feenix:**

**The Black Butterfly Trilogy
(Two Preview Chapters)**

Dante' Feenix

Chapter One

Caterpillar

His name was Nadet'… pronounced Na-day. Nadet S. Efil, the man of many symbols, an 11 year old boy's self given moniker. Nadet has always felt that everything around us and everything that happens to us were symbolic of something much more significant.   That's probably why he used a lot of parables and symbols to illustrate his points without even realizing it… like the caterpillar and the butterfly for instance. Many great men in history did this, even Jesus… thought Nadet to himself.

Jesus used parables to teach his disciples and illustrate his lessons to everyone. Nadet learned that in bible study, so often he wondered why most people looked at him as if he were crazy. His grandmother always said, "It's because you're not Jesus by any stretch of the imagination and wouldn't want to fill those shoes if somebody gave'm to ya!" Well... even with that in mind, Nadet still believed the butterfly and caterpillar were significant symbols that spoke volumes about all of us.

The butterfly represented change and freedom. The "change" is the transformation it makes from caterpillar to butterfly once it matures. The "freedom" is the ability to hit its potential of flight once transformed. We all have a longing to fly inside of us but fear the change or cocoon that maturity brings. You see, the cocoon represents the death of the caterpillar (who we are) and the birth of the butterfly (who we are destined to be). Most of us are scared to die that's why we don't fly.

This reminded Nadet of his mother, the first caterpillar he ever saw and his inspiration to fly or as she liked to say, "Hit my maximum potential." Just one look at her or one conversation with her and it became obvious that she was a star. However, like most people, she let the circumstances of life like bills, negative opinions, and the responsibility of having a child stop her from becoming a butterfly.

His mother was young, beautiful, and full of life! All she ever wanted to do was become a model or an actress. What could be wrong with that? She was one of the first models of what was sure to become one of the largest African-American modeling agencies in the country, but she just couldn't get the big break she was looking for. You know, the one that stops you from working a day job! She modeled part-time, worked part-time, went to school part-time, but was out of her mind all the time! To Nadet and many others, his mom had everything anyone needed to be a top actress, model, or whatever she wanted to be. A hot ticket, if ever there was one. As a matter of fact, the only thing she didn't have was real support from her friends and family.

Even though everyone begged Eboni to be in fashion shows and guys would give their right lung to date her, she still needed something concrete to validate her destiny; something like a big modeling job, contract, or movie would have been nice. It wasn't easy facing the constant nagging of family and friends.

"Modeling is just a dream."

"You need a full time job girl!"

Although that may sound like good advice to most, without any real words of encouragement, it can kill your dreams especially when she also faced the constant rejection of auditions.

Also everyone was the same. They could tell that Eboni was different and no one would have been surprised if they had seen her on television but they really didn't want her to make it! When it looked like her talent was going to take her somewhere they couldn't go, they would use conventional thinking to keep her from reaching for more. You know how it goes; use the obstacles that are part of everyday life to make a person second-guess their destiny.

Just because modeling was not a real option for them, they acted like it wasn't a real option for her. She was five feet, ten inches tall without heels, a natural size two, and had long jet-black hair. Telling her that modeling or acting was just a dream, was like telling a kid with tons of athletic ability and a nice jump shot, that he has a one percent chance of making it to the NBA. That may sound like good advice at first, unless that kid's name is Michael Jordan. People really need to check themselves when giving advice because they just create obstacles, never offering solutions. One thing was clear to Nadet for sure, "People will mess you up in life, if you let them!"

Eboni was a true artist... crazy as hell! Nadet was glad she stopped listening to negative people because tomorrow they were going to another one of her auditions. His mother usually took him because Nadet was her good luck charm and she was going to need it. She would be auditioning for the first all black soap opera produced by John James, the hottest television producer out there. He was white, but cool because Nadet liked most of his other shows. Nadet's mom was going to need her A-game though because John James was the best, and if she got this role it would be history.

Chapter Two

A Star Is Born

"History in the making, I'm going to be a superstar!"

"Okay superstar, but do all of us a favor, sit your pretty ass down somewhere and shut the hell up!"

"Kiss my entire ass, Earl!"

"Ma stop! Get down from there. You look crazy."

Nadet grabbed his Ma's arm and pulled her down from the window's sill as Earl continued to yell.

"That's what I'm talking 'bout! Bring that fine ass down here girl. I got something for it!"

"This block is so ghetto," Nadet said, as he shook his head and his Ma attempted to explain why she was so excited about her upcoming audition.

"If I get this role and it's successful, this could be the first of many black soap operas which could open the doors for black actors everywhere, Day-Day."

"Okay Ma, but let's just start with you first, focus. I know that you are going to make it this time. I can just feel it, but if you don't, I'm here. We can just go somewhere else. We've waited in a thousand lines before and I'll wait in a thousand more until somebody picks you."

His mother looked like an angel as the light from the street lamps illuminated her from behind as she said, "I never thought that the man of my dreams would come from inside of me."

Huh? There she goes talking crazy again.

After Eboni got dressed they drove down to the casting agency. There were already about a thousand people standing against the wall along the building. Everyone in line looked like they were showing off, just trying to scare away the competition. They were singing, dancing, over acting, and just plain looking stupid. When Nadet and his mother got out of the car everyone immediately began to watch them. That happened all the time because his mom was so tall and striking in heels, plus he was with her. People could never understand why she would bring a kid on an audition, but he knew how to be quiet and stay out of the way. As they walked pass everyone two women in the background said, "Where in the hell does she think she's going?

"She better get to the back of the line like everybody else, fake ass Iman."

There's always one or two at every audition, you know, women that hate on other women. Nadet knew his mom must have heard them just as he had so he wondered why she didn't say something back. He was so sick of people saying what they wanted to them and getting away with it. After going to the counter at the front of the line, Eboni walked right into the office and turned to Nadet.

"Wait here baby. Wish me luck."

"Good luck ma, but do I have to wait out here?"

"Don't worry, I'll be right back."

Damn, now all these people were upset and looking at me just because she didn't have to wait in line. I didn't do anything, I'm just here, Nadet thought to himself.

After about five minutes the two women that called Nadet's mother a fake ass Iman came to the front of the line and one asked the receptionist, "Why are we still in line while other people can just go in?" They looked at him and stretched their eyes wide open while they were asking the question. Suddenly before the receptionist could answer, the office door flung open and Eboni emerged from the darkness of the studio yelling, "It's called an appointment bitch! Get one the next time you try to audition for something." She stood boldly placing her hands on her hips and continued, "En' you betta get outta my baby's face, before your first one be at a doctor's office! What? You got somethin' to say?"

"No, we wasn't even talking about ya'll."

"That's what I thought; I don't have time for this."

Oh yeah, she didn't look like it but that eastside Baltimore project chick would come out of her if you messed with her family... especially her son. She grabbed Nadet's hand as they strolled pass everyone and said, "We the shit now Day-Day, I got the role!" After they did the cabbage patch in the parking lot, Eboni got down on one knee and hugged Nadet, "Nobody believed in me but you. Shit, I didn't even believe in myself."

"That's because they don't know who you are, ma. You can do anything. That's what you always told me."

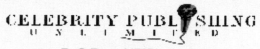

CELEBRITY PUBLISHING
UNLIMITED

P. O Box 66595
Baltimore, Maryland 21239

Order Form

Name: _____

Address:_____

City _____ State _____ Zip _____

Qty	Title	Price	Total
	Diary Of A 12 Inch Brotha	$15.00	
	Black Butterfly	12.00	
	Black Butterfly 2	12.00	
	Black Butterfly 3	12.00	
	Available On Amazon Kindle		
	Split Ya Wig, BB4	12.00	
	- Coming Soon Amazon Kindle -		
	The Ruler's Back		
	Blaque Barbees		
		Subtotal	
		Shipping	
	...Shipping charges... Ground First Book ....$3.85 Each additional book............$1.50	**Total**	$_____

Make Institutional Check or Money Orders payable to:
Dante' Feenix

CELEBRITY PUBLISHING
U N L I M I T E D

P. O Box 66595
Baltimore, Maryland 21239

Order Form

Name: _____

Address:_____

City _____ State _____ Zip _____

Qty	Title	Price	Total
	Diary Of A 12 Inch Brotha	$15.00	
	Black Butterfly	12.00	
	Black Butterfly 2	12.00	
	Black Butterfly 3	12.00	
	Available On Amazon Kindle		
	Split Ya Wig, BB4	12.00	
	- Coming Soon Amazon Kindle -		
	The Ruler's Back		
	Blaque Barbees		
		Subtotal	
		Shipping	
	...Shipping charges...	**Total**	$
	Ground First Book $3.85		
	Each additional book...................$1.50		

Make Institutional Check or Money Orders payable to:
Dante' Feenix